THE SIGN
OF THE SCORPION

The Moon of Masarrah Series, Book Two

FARAH ZAMAN

ISBN: 978-1-945873-14-0

The Moon of Masarrah Series, Book Two
The Moon of Masarrah Series, Book One, is available wherever books are sold.

Bulk purchases are available for schools and groups.
For information, please email the author at Zefarah@gmail.com

Production managed by Niyah Press
www.niyahpress.com

Cover Design by Anis Puteri

First and Foremost,
My praise and gratitude to the One
Who taught me by the Pen.

To my family
who is always my safe harbor in the storms of life.

And for all
who assisted in reading and sharing their thoughts,
my sincere thanks and appreciation.
I couldn't have embarked on this odyssey without you.

Prologue

NIGHT SHROUDED THE oasis in gathering veils of darkness, chasing away the lingering twilight and lulling its dwellers into slumber. As midnight approached, a playful wind blew in from the far reaches of the desert, gleefully skittering sand in its path and tickling the date palms with mischievous fingers. Except for the moths fluttering at the lanterns and the beating of bats' wings, all was silent as the lone woman blended with the shadows and walked on soundless feet towards the darkness beyond.

She glanced at the skies above. Stars glimmered like scattered jewels and a lazy moon snoozed behind a thick blanket of clouds. Tonight, the beauty of the night was lost upon her. Her thoughts were on the stolen bracelet and the web of intrigue she now found herself in. As she approached her destination, she saw a warm glow at the top of the dark edifice. The one who had summoned her was waiting. Hastening her strides, she reached the door and opened it.

Entering, she shined a flashlight onto a long flight of stairs. It was narrow and steep, twisting upwards in a spiral. As she stared at the daunting length, the woman was tempted to turn back and return to her bed. But she had come this far and must continue on. Her distressing dilemma had to be dealt with once and for all. Taking a deep breath, she gripped the railing and began to climb, her slippers echoing on the ancient stone stairs.

When she reached the top, the summoner stepped out of the shadows, silhouetted in the glare of a candle beyond. "You're here at last. I was beginning to think you wouldn't come."

"I almost turned back," said the woman. "I hated dragging myself out of bed in the middle of the night. Why all this secrecy? Is it really necessary?"

"I wanted to be away from prying eyes and ears. Come, let's sit down and talk."

The woman entered the room and was gripped with a strange sense of foreboding. The writhing shadows seemed thick with menace and she felt an eerie sensation of danger, like someone waited to pounce on her in the dark. Her eyes searched the gloom, looking for she knew not what. Except for herself and the one who had summoned her, the room was empty. She shivered and drew her shawl closer as a cool draft blew in from the open window. Silently chiding herself for her foolish imaginings, she pulled a chair and sat down.

Looking her summoner in the eye, she said, "There's nothing more to talk about. You know my ultimatum. Either return the bracelet tomorrow or I'll tell the family you stole it."

"Of course, I'll return it. I wanted to make sure you haven't told anyone about it."

"I told you I wouldn't. Your secret is safe as long as you return it."

"I want you to swear you told no one I took it."

"I swear by Allah I haven't told a single soul it was you."

"Now swear you've told no one you were meeting me here tonight."

"I swear by Allah no one knows I'm here."

"Then I have nothing to fear," murmured the summoner.

"You'll return the bracelet tomorrow?"

"Yes, you won't have to worry about that ever again."

"I'm glad to hear that." The woman stood up. "I'll return now. It's been a tiring day."

"Wait, there's something I want to show you before you go."

"What is it?"

"It's in the bag by the window. Let me get it."

The summoner went across to the window, glanced out and stood still. "Someone's coming down the path. They must have seen the light."

"Who can it be?" said the woman.

"I don't know. Come, see if you can tell who it is."

The summoner moved aside, and the woman took a few hesitant steps towards the window. Before she reached it, she came to a stop. She was filled with that nameless fear again. She stared at the wide opening, reluctant to go any closer to the gaping void. Was someone really down there? She tilted her head, her ears straining for a sound. She could only hear the erratic beating of her heart. All of a sudden, she felt like fleeing as fast as her feet would allow.

As she stood poised for flight, the hairs on her nape rose. She gave a strangled cry as a pair of cruel arms grabbed her from behind. She knew her life was in peril as she was dragged towards the window. Her desperate cries filled the air as she struggled for her freedom. She kicked and butted her head against her captor, digging her nails into the hands that held her like a vise. Even though she fought with desperation, she was no match for her aggressor. They had reached the window.

"Please," she sobbed. "Please let me go. I won't say anything about the bracelet."

"It's too late," came the cold voice of her summoner. "You shouldn't have interfered."

The next moment, she was lifted over the window sill. She felt herself dangling over empty air. She gave a shrill scream of panic, her fingers clutching for a handhold and her feet thrashing in a frenzy beneath her. The arms released their hold. A long shriek of terror left her throat as she hurtled to the ground below with dizzying speed. Before blessed oblivion overtook her, she realized with fleeting clarity that she had been deceived and was on her way to meet death.

Chapter One
Desert Castle

L AYLA HORANI PEERED out the window of the seesawing jetliner, eager to catch her first glimpse of the Republic of Ghassan. The swaying aircraft banked sharply to the right and the clouds parted to reveal a curving mass of land verged by turquoise waters.

"I see land." Layla turned her shining green eyes to her friend Zahra Alkurdi, who sat next to her. "We're here at last."

"We sure are," said Zahra, with an unmistakable British accent, a wide smile on her face.

She and Layla were both fourteen. Layla was tall and slender while Zahra was shorter with dark eyes and chubby cheeks.

Behind them, Layla's brother Adam, said, "That water looks wonderful."

"Yes, good enough to swim in," said Zaid with the same British accent as his sister Zahra.

The boys were a year older than the girls. Adam had a square face and hair that had a tendency to look tousled. Zaid's face was longer, and he wore his dark hair cut close to his head.

The teenagers had met due to the friendship between their

fathers. The two men, hailing from Midan, had become friends while at college in the United States. Zaid and Zahra's father had gone on to pursue a doctorate in history in England. Layla and Adam's father had remained in the United States to study medicine. The two men had gotten married around the same time and settled down in their adopted countries. Three years prior, Professor Alkurdi returned to Midan to become head of the history department at Crescent City University.

Layla smiled as she remembered their first meeting with Zaid and Zahra. It had been at her grandfather's home in Midan last year. Layla and Adam had been visiting there for the first time and their father had invited Zaid and Zahra to keep them company. During their vacation at Bayan House, the teenagers had become fast friends while chasing after pirates and searching for the long-lost Moon of Masarrah diamond. Though fluent in Arabic, they reverted to their first language of English when they were together.

As Layla straightened her beige scarf and dusted crumbs off her olive-green tunic, a tingle of anticipation shot through her. It had been almost a year since Shaykh Sulaiman ibn Al-Khalili had invited them to visit Dukhan Oasis, his desert home in Ghassan. She and Adam had set off from San Francisco four days ago, making a detour in Midan to visit their grandfather. Earlier that Tuesday afternoon, they had met up with Zaid and Zahra to catch the one-hour flight to Ghassan. Now, only minutes away from landing, Layla could hardly sit still.

THEY WERE MET at the Ghassan International Airport by Mustapha, the Shaykh's employee. They had become acquainted with him last year when he had accompanied the Shaykh to Bayan House. He was a strapping man with the face of a Sumo wrestler and the build of a boxer. He was dressed in jeans and a tightfitting T-shirt that bared the rippling muscles of his brown arms. He escorted them to a burgundy Honda Pilot and soon, they were speeding along on a busy highway.

"The oasis is in Rukan Province," he told them. "It's four hours away. We should get there about nine this evening, *insha Allah.*"

"It's too bad there wasn't an earlier flight from Midan," said Zaid. "We would have reached the oasis sooner."

"It doesn't matter," said Adam. "I think it's better traveling in the afternoon."

"This is the first time you're all visiting Ghassan?" asked Mustapha.

"No, Zaid and I have been to Ghassan City a couple of times before," said Zahra.

"That's where I live," said Mustapha. "It's very beautiful."

"I'd love to see Ghassan City," said Adam. "Maybe when our parents come, we can all go together."

"How are the twins, Hassan and Hakeem?" asked Mustapha.

"They were disappointed they couldn't come with us," said Layla. She felt a pang of regret when she thought of her younger brothers. "But they would have driven us crazy. It's for the best."

Mustapha laughed. "From what I saw of them last year, they looked like a handful."

"They'll be coming with our parents the last week of our vacation," said Adam, "so they'll get to see the oasis."

"Our parents will be coming at the same time too," said Zahra. "They'll be flying straight from Malaysia." Professor and Mrs. Alkurdi did a lecture tour in a different country every year. This year was no exception.

"Are you looking forward to your vacation at the oasis?" asked Mustapha.

"Oh yes," said Adam. "We'll enjoy being so close to nature."

"Does the Shaykh have a house there?" asked Zaid.

Mustapha chuckled. "I guess you could say that. He never told you?"

"No, we never thought to ask," said Layla.

"Then I won't spoil the surprise," said the chauffeur.

"Dukhan Oasis," Layla murmured. "The Oasis of Smoke. It's such a dreamy name."

"You'll have your fill of it for six weeks," said Mustapha. "By then, you'll be glad to get back to the concrete jungle."

He went on to tell them about the relatives he would be spending the night with in Khaldun, the nearest city to Dukhan Oasis.

Two hours later, they left the crowded highway. They were now journeying across landscape that alternated between sandy plains, desolate gray hills, and unexpected patches of greenery. Layla leaned back and closed her eyes. She wondered for the umpteenth time what the oasis would be like. Her daydream conjured up a fertile tract of land abundant with date palms, herds of camels and flowing water springs. As they came closer to their destination, the sun sank to the west amidst a vivid carpet of vermilion clouds. The orange and red hues reminded Layla of an artist's palette.

"Almost there," Mustapha murmured as darkness began to etch itself on the landscape around them.

The teenagers stared out at the roadway. At the sides, were limestone hills that cast long shadows ahead. As they turned a curve, a most unexpected sight met their eyes. A sprawling castle stood before them like a medieval stronghold, its lines thrown into sharp relief by the luminous full moon.

"Welcome to Dukhan Castle," said Mustapha.

In her wildest imagination Layla would have never guessed they were coming to a remote desert castle. "Wow, this is unreal," she said, blown away by the fact that they would be staying at an honest to goodness castle.

"Awesome," said Zahra.

"Cool," said Adam.

"Wicked," said Zaid.

Mustapha chuckled. "The castle does take people by surprise. The Shaykh prefers living here than anywhere else. He's very reclusive. I guess it's his Bedouin roots."

The Honda stopped before steel gates and Mustapha reached a thick arm out the window to punch in a code on the security panel. The gates swung open and they drove into a forecourt lined with date palms. To the left was a parking lot filled with several vehicles. They came to a stop next to a sporty red Saab. The ultra-modern conveyance seemed out of place in a setting like this.

They stepped out of the vehicle and Layla stared in fascination at the castle's facade. The monumental square structure towered several stories into the air and stretched across the horizon. At each end rose a rounded tower. A porch-like covering with arch-shaped columns ran along the entire front. She knew it was called a portico. She had seen them on many buildings.

As she stared up at the dark windows, Layla saw a faint movement on the third floor. A woman wearing allover white was looking down at them, her eyes like sooty smudges above her veil. She stood still for several seconds before disappearing with a quick movement. Layla blinked. If she had believed in ghosts, the woman in white would have certainly passed for one.

"Don't worry about your luggage," said Mustapha. "The servants will take them up to your rooms."

At the front door, Mustapha rang the bell. Moments later it opened, and a plump manservant clad in a black uniform peered out at them. He was in his early sixties, with iron-gray hair and overhanging brows.

After *salaams* were exchanged, Mustapha said, "This is Dhul Fikar, the butler. He'll take care of you from here."

Dhul Fikar opened the door wide. "Welcome. Please come inside."

"I'll say goodbye for now," said Mustapha to the teenagers. "As I told you, my relatives in Khaldun are expecting me. I'll spend the night there and return to Ghassan City. Enjoy your vacation and I'll see you soon, *insha Allah.*"

The teenagers thanked him warmly before following the butler through a wide entryway. It opened into a cavernous domed hall with a magnificent chandelier hanging from the center and gold and silver brocade curtains at the windows. Several low couches with ottomans were laid in a circle around a Turkish rug. A coffee table stood in the middle, bearing a crystal vase filled with flowers. The fresh blooms scented the air with a delicate perfume.

Dhul Fikar gestured to the couches. "Please have a seat. I'll inform the family of your arrival."

After the butler left, Layla said, "Isn't this place amazing? It looks like a castle out of a fairy tale."

Zahra grinned. "Let's hope there's no wicked witch or wizard here."

Minutes later, a woman entered the domed hall. She was in her mid-forties, dressed in a brown gown and cream scarf. Bright, inquisitive eyes were set above a rather pointed nose. She reminded Layla of an eager bird.

She said in a slightly guttural voice, "I'm Ghazala, Shaykh Sulaiman's cousin. Welcome to Dukhan Castle. It's a pleasure to meet you all. My cousin has spoken very well of you. I'm afraid he's unable to welcome you here himself. But you'll meet him tomorrow. Now, tell me your names."

As the teenagers introduced themselves, a woman clad in all-black *hijab* hurried into the domed hall.

"Ah, here's Nura," said Ghazala. "She's going to be your maid during your stay here."

We're getting our own maid?

Nura was in her early twenties, with a small cherubic face

and large dark eyes. She seemed very serious for such a young woman.

"Nura will take you to the dining room," said Ghazala. "We've prepared a late dinner for you. I hope you enjoy it. I'll be waiting for you here when you're done."

"Please follow me," said Nura, beckoning to them with a tiny hand.

She led them to a dining room with a long mahogany table. Layla counted sixteen chairs around it. Suspended above the table was an antique crystal chandelier. Layla's stomach growled when she smelled the delicious flavors wafting out from the chafing dishes.

"You can wash up in the bathroom across the hallway," the maid said, her voice soft and low. "When you're ready to eat, just lift the covers and help yourselves. I'll be back when you're done."

After their tiring journey, the warm lamb stew, grilled beef *kofta* and a delicious dessert of *kanafeh* were eaten with enthusiasm. At the end of the meal, the maid led them back to the domed hall. Ghazala was thumbing through a magazine. "Sit down," she said to them. "I'm afraid the time has now come for me to be the bearer of some bad tidings." She looked at them with grave eyes.

"What is it?" Adam shared an anxious look with the others.

"Unfortunately, the House of Al-Khalili has suffered a tragic loss. Sulaiman's son, Rashid, died in the desert a month ago. As a result, my cousin became ill and had a stroke. Fortunately, it was a mild one. He's able to speak but is still weak and finds it difficult to move."

"Oh no," said Layla, her eyes wide with dismay. "That's awful."

"Why didn't someone tell us?" said Zaid. "We could have canceled our trip."

"Sulaiman wouldn't hear of it. He said you had been looking

forward to this visit for almost a year and would be very disappointed if it was called off. Because of the circumstances, the tragedy wasn't publicized. Only the family and trusted employees know of it."

"Poor Shaykh Sulaiman," said Zahra. "Will we be able to visit him?"

"Yes, he has requested you visit him in the morning after breakfast. The meal is served from seven to ten in the sunroom. As for the other meals, lunch is at twelve and dinner at seven. Both are served in the dining room where you just ate. For dinner, we take extra care to dress our best. You must remember that. Now, Nura will take you up to your rooms. I'll see you all in the morning."

The maid took them up a stairway and through a maze of hallways. She opened a door which led into another long hallway.

"These are the *Ghaf* Suites," she told them. "They're named after the grove of *ghaf* trees outside your windows."

"What's a *ghaf* tree?" asked Adam.

"The *ghaf* is an evergreen tree that grows well in deserts. If there should be a fire, the nearest stairway is down the hallway and leads to the *ghaf* grove. The stairway only opens from inside and is locked on the outside. You can use it to go out, but you won't be able to get in unless you prop it open. But we don't keep doors propped open in these parts. Small creatures can get inside and cause havoc. You'll remember that, won't you?"

They all nodded, and the maid continued, "Four suites have been prepared for you. You can choose which one you'd like. They're all the same. The other suites in this wing will be made ready for your family when they come. You'll be the only ones here for now. If you need to get in touch with me, all the rooms have an intercom hooked up to the servants' lounge. You can leave a message there. *Masah al-khair.*"

Layla heaved a sigh after the maid left. "I wish we'd come at a better time."

"We'll just have to make the best of things," said Zahra. "Let's choose our suites. I can hardly keep my eyes open."

Later that night, as Layla lay on the verge of sleep, she recalled Ghazala's words: "Because of the circumstances, the tragedy wasn't publicized." What had she meant by "circumstances?" It seemed strange to keep someone's death a secret. *I guess we'll soon find out what it is.* Her thoughts came to a halt as she fell asleep.

It seemed to Layla she had just closed her eyes when she was awakened by a bone-chilling scream.

Chapter Two
The House of Al-Khalili

IT WAS A long drawn out wail of deep anguish that seem to go on forever. Layla stared at the darkness around her, her heart pounding and shivers running up and down her spine as the frightful sound vibrated on the air. After the last note faded away, her heartbeat returned to normal. *What in the world was that?* It had sounded like someone in pain. But it could not have been. It must have been a wild animal from the desert, wandering outside the castle walls. Convinced this was what she had heard, Layla turned on her side and fell asleep once more.

THE NEXT MORNING, Layla looked around with pleasure at her suite. Zahra had chosen the first one, Zaid the second, Adam the third, and Layla the last one. Her suite was painted a soft tangerine color, with blue and white Moroccan tiles in the bathroom. The single window at the back was hung with opulent, grayish red curtains that Layla recognized as damask. They had a couch at home with the same covering. She pulled the drapes aside, eager to see her surroundings in the light of day. Behind the meshed window screen, she saw the limbs of a tree. *It must be one of those ghaf trees the maid told us about. So much for a room with a view.*

Before they headed down to breakfast, Adam asked, "Did anyone hear a scream last night?"

"Yes, I did," said Layla.

Zaid nodded. "I heard it too"

"And so did I," said Zahra.

"It must have been an animal," said Layla.

"It sounded like a woman screaming to me," said Adam.

"Some animals sound very human," said Zaid. "It must have been a jackal or a hyena."

"It was too close for comfort," said Layla. "I'm glad there's a wall around the castle to keep those wild animals out."

When they descended the stairway to the first floor, Layla could not help thinking how creepy the inside of the castle was. The narrow windows hardly let in enough light and the place was simply humongous. The ceilings seemed to soar a mile high and the hallways were wide and long.

They ran into Dhul Fikar, the butler from last night, who escorted them to the sunroom.

"Oh, how nice," said Layla, looking with delight at the room.

The outside wall was made of glass, with vines and climbing plants running across the surface. Morning sunlight streamed through gaps in the foliage, casting dancing sunbeams onto the ceramic floor tiles. Like the dining room, a long table stood in the center. On both sides of the room were sideboards, one holding a microwave, toaster and beverage urns while the other had fruits and steaming platters of food. Ghazala and another woman were the only ones there.

"There you are," said Ghazala. This morning she wore a green floral scarf and a black gown that flowed loosely over her pudgy body. "I would like to introduce you to Mrs. Haddad, the tutor. Mariam, these are the young guests I was telling you about."

Mrs. Haddad was in her mid-forties, with a long, gaunt face. Her dark hair was twisted into a knot at the back of her neck and there was a reserved expression on her face. Layla wondered who was being tutored by this rather stern-looking woman. *We really have no idea who else lives here. I suppose we'll find out soon enough.*

"I'm pleased to meet you," said Mrs. Haddad in English, with a crisp British accent. She did not seem big on breakfast and after pouring herself a mug of coffee, she left.

"Help yourselves to whatever you like," said Ghazala. "At ten, Sulaiman's personal assistant will be waiting for you in the domed hall to take you to see my cousin. You have a whole hour. There's no need to rush. The rest of the family should be here soon."

A youth came in while they were eating. He was about eighteen, tall and lanky of build. Unlike some tall teenagers who tended to slouch, he carried himself ramrod straight. He had chiseled features topped by thick, curly hair.

"This is Tariq, the Shaykh's grandson," said Ghazala. "In fact, he's the Shaykh's only grandchild."

Really? I don't know why I thought the Shaykh would have dozens of grandkids. Guess I was wrong.

"Welcome," said Tariq. "We're happy to have you here."

Layla wondered if it was his father who had died. It would account for the sad expression in his eyes. A girl wearing jeans and a blue striped blouse walked into the room next. She was about fifteen, with flashing dark eyes and frizzy hair hanging loose below her shoulders. She would have been quite pretty if not for the discontented droop of her mouth.

"This is Hala," said Ghazala. "Her father and stepmother are also cousins of Sulaiman. Where are they, Hala? I thought they would be here by now."

The girl shrugged. "*Abu* went for a ride and Mama Suha has a headache." Her voice was whiny, and she said "Mama Suha" with a scornful curl of her lips.

"I suppose our guests will meet them later," said Ghazala. "That leaves only Faisal."

"I hear the sweet sound of my name," said a pleasant baritone, and a man sauntered into the sunroom. The butter knife slipped out of Layla's hand as she stared at the newcomer. Dressed in jeans and a white T-shirt, he was strikingly handsome with hazel eyes, a smooth-shaven face and the same dark, curly hair as Tariq. He was in his late twenties and wore a brooding expression on his face, like some hero from a gothic novel. He seemed to fit right into the atmosphere of the castle.

As Layla picked up the knife again, she could not help being amused at herself when she recalled the story of Joseph in the *Qur'an*. The women of the city had been bowled over by his beauty when they saw him. They had ended up cutting their hands on the knives they had been peeling fruit with. *I'm not so different from those women.*

"This is Faisal," said Ghazala. "He's also Sulaiman's cousin."

Faisal studied them for a moment before saying, "Welcome. I hope you have fun running around this old pile of stones. If you should get bored, I'm sure Tariq will tell you of all the wonderful entertainments awaiting you in the desert."

There was a slight sarcasm in his tone and Tariq's lips tightened, though the youth remained silent. After getting her food, Hala seated herself next to Tariq, smiling at him and speaking to him in a low voice. Faisal took only coffee and toast, which he ate in moody silence.

Turning to the teenagers, Ghazala asked, "How do you like your rooms?"

AFTER BREAKFAST, THE teenagers went to the domed hall to await the Shaykh's personal assistant. A tall, trim man walked in a few minutes later. He was in his early forties, with tinges of gray at the temples and an olive tint to his skin. A long, intelligent face and deep, penetrating eyes gave him an air of quiet capability.

"I'm Kareem, Shaykh Sulaiman's personal assistant," he said in a gravelly voice. "Come, I'll take you to the Shaykh's suite."

They followed him to a spacious chamber on the other side of the ground floor. In the sitting room, they were met by a man who wore a uniform of white pants and a white short-sleeved shirt.

"This is Qais, the Shaykh's nurse," said Kareem. "He'll take you to see the Shaykh. I'll see you later."

Qais was unlike any nurse Layla had ever seen. She judged him somewhere in his forties. A large head and wide shoulders tapered down to a short, squat body and a pair of massive hands.

"Please come with me," he said. His voice sounded like a low rumble of thunder. "The Shaykh is waiting for you."

He led them into a cool and dim bedchamber. An overhead fan whirred gently above and white roman shades blocked out the brilliant sunlight at a long row of windows. Gesturing to the wide four-poster bed, Qais withdrew, closing the door behind him.

Shaykh Sulaiman was resting against the pillows, covered waist down by a white coverlet. His hands lay limply at the sides and he looked thin and frail. Sparse white hair was neatly combed while his beard and moustache were well-groomed. His bronze skin had a sickly, grayish cast to it.

He said in a slurred voice, "*Marhaban*. Welcome to my desert home. I'm very happy to see you all again. I'm a bit helpless at the moment, as you can see."

"Shaykh Sulaiman, Auntie Ghazala told us about your son's death," said Layla. "We're very sorry to hear about it."

The Shaykh's lips quivered, and his chest began to heave with silent sobs. Tears rolled down his sunken cheeks as he gave in to his grief. Adam and Zaid took hold of his wrinkled hands, offering comfort. A lump formed in Layla's throat and she felt the burn of tears in her eyes as she watched the painful scene. At last, the Shaykh regained his composure.

"You must pardon me," he said, reaching for a tissue and blotting his tears. "Nothing happens except by Allah's will, but losing Rashid was a painful blow. I'm learning to accept it day by day. Unfortunately, I'm unable to join you for meals or other activities. But you must make yourselves at home. I wish you to become friends with my grandson, Tariq. His father was my eldest son, but he and his wife were killed in an accident a few years ago..." the Shaykh's voice trailed away. He shook his head, as if to chase away an unpleasant memory. "Now my other son, Rashid, is gone too and I have no more children left. Tariq is my only remaining heir. He's taken his uncle's death hard, for they were very close. I hope your visit will cheer him up. We have a recreation area that you'll find quite entertaining. You can use it anytime you wish. I want you to enjoy your stay here."

"Don't worry about us," said Adam. "We'll be fine."

THE TEENAGERS SPENT the rest of the morning unpacking their suitcases and organizing their personal items for easy access. At lunch, they met Hala's father, Miftah, and her stepmother, Suha. Miftah was in his early forties, beardless and broad of shoulders. A high forehead gave way to bushy eyebrows and a prominent nose. His close-fitting Polo shirt did nothing to disguise the roll of fat around his middle.

In a voice that had a gruff quality to it, he said, "Welcome to Dukhan Castle. I hope you enjoy your visit."

In her mid-twenties, Suha was much younger than her husband. She wore a scarf and had sculpted features set in a heart-shaped face. Her eyes were fringed by the longest eyelashes Layla had ever seen.

"I hope you like it here," she said. "We've never had such young guests before."

Ghazala pointed to the side of the table that backed the windows and told the teenagers, "Sit on that side. The family will be on the other side. It will be easier to converse with you that way. Kareem and Mrs. Haddad dine with us in the evenings at my cousin's request. We'll be a larger group at dinner."

It's very considerate of the Shaykh to let the PA and tutor have dinner with the family.

After the family were seated, the two chairs at the head and foot of the table remained empty. Layla realized Shaykh Sulaiman must have sat at the head and his dead son, Rashid, at the foot. The sight of the empty chairs tugged at her heart. *Life has the tendency to leave behind a lot of empty chairs.*

As they were eating, Ghazala said to the family, "I received a phone call from Jumana earlier. She'll be coming tomorrow. We'll be having refreshments in the domed hall when she arrives." Looking across at the teenagers she said, "You young people are welcome to join us."

"Thank you," said Layla. *Who's Jumana?*

"I'm glad she's coming," said Tariq, his sad eyes lighting up. "It's been too long since she was here."

"She must be disappointed she's no longer going to be the lady of the castle," said Faisal, the handsome, moody cousin they'd met at breakfast.

"It's a pity she didn't get married before going abroad to university," said Miftah. "Now look what's happened. I wouldn't let Hala wait so long. Girls need to marry young or they become old maids."

Oh no, he didn't say that. Some women would tear him to bits if they heard him.

"I hope you're not going to marry Hala off before she finishes university," said Faisal.

Miftah looked annoyed. "You're the last person I would take advice from about marriage."

Faisal threw his cousin a resentful look. "I might have known you'd bring that up."

Bring what up?

"Then don't act like you're some marriage expert," said Miftah. "What if Hala gets married before she finishes university? Is that a crime? Should I tell her no if she meets someone and doesn't want to wait? Should I, Hala?"

A mysterious smile played on Hala's lips. "Of course not, *Abu.*"

"See?" said Miftah. "Hala will make her own decision when she's ready."

"Fine," said Faisal. "It's her life."

"*Abu,* Uncle Saad sent me a text earlier," said Hala. "He wants to know when we'll be going to Ghassan City. He promised to take me shopping."

Suha was the one who answered her stepdaughter. "Hala, we can't go yet. Your uncle Sulaiman is still very ill."

Hala's eyes flashed with anger. "I wasn't talking to you."

Suha's face stiffened and she looked down at her plate, red spots on her cheeks.

Miftah turned to frown at his daughter. "Hala, you will apologize to Mama Suha."

Hala scowled. "Why should I? She's always jumping in when I'm speaking to you."

Miftah's face became red. "Hala, you will apologize to Mama Suha now or leave the table."

"Why are you taking her side?" said Hala. "You care more for her than you care for me. I'm going to ask Uncle Saad to take me to live with him in Ghassan City. Then you'll be sorry."

With those words, she shoved back her chair and ran out of the room.

"Silly child," said Ghazala. "As if that uncle of hers could be bothered."

Faisal grinned, his teeth showing white against his golden tan. "Hala is such a brat. She reminds me of myself at that age. I was allowed to run wild just like her."

Miftah coughed as he almost choked on a piece of chicken. "Allowed to run wild?" His eyebrows looked like thunderclouds. "What do you mean by that?"

"You've spoiled the girl, what else?"

"I have not." Miftah's voice was so forceful that flecks of food flew from his mouth. "It's been hard for her, losing her mother at such a young age. She's still grieving."

"You need to take a firmer hand with her," said Ghazala. "Her tantrums are getting worse."

"It's easy for you to say," said Miftah. "You don't have children of your own. You don't know what it's like."

"*Khalas*. Enough," said Ghazala, her tone sharp. "Sulaiman will be angry if he hears of these disagreements at the table. You know what he'll do if he becomes angry, don't you?"

What would he do? I can't imagine what they have to fear from that gentle, soft-spoken man.

THE TEENAGERS SPENT the rest of the afternoon in their rooms. They still felt a bit tired from their flight and the long drive to the castle. Before Layla knew it, it was time for dinner. Remembering Ghazala's advice, she donned a violet floral dress, pinning the matching scarf with a pearl cluster brooch. She did not usually make a fuss with her appearance and stuck with a few tried and true outfits, much to the despair of her mother. She was glad now for the summer dresses she had brought. They would come in handy for all the dinners ahead. *Thank you, Mom.*

When they went down to the dining room, the PA and the tutor were there, and a strange man was sitting next to Ghazala.

"This is my husband, Bilal," said Ghazala to the teenagers. "He's working on a new research project. He's been very busy lately."

Husband? I didn't even think she had one. I'm sure she didn't mention him before.

Bilal was a man of unremarkable appearance in his late forties. He had a hooked nose, a small goatee and shoulders that were a bit hunched. With his thick glasses and balding pate, he looked like an owl. He seemed ill at ease among the gathering.

"Welcome." He bestowed a brief smile on them. "It's a pleasure to meet you."

I almost expected to hear him hoot.

Ghazala, who was wearing a beautifully embroidered black *abaya,* said, "Where's Hala?"

"She won't be dining with us this evening," said Miftah. He did not offer an explanation, and no one asked for one.

He must have given her a timeout for that tantrum at lunch.

Layla glanced over at Hala's stepmother. Suha was dressed in a maroon caftan, her beige scarf pinned with a lovely, silver filigree diamond pin. A touch of *kohl* brightened her eyes, highlighting the amazing length of her lashes. She looked relaxed.

She's probably enjoying the reprieve from her snarky stepdaughter.

"Where's Faisal?" Ghazala asked next.

"Dhul Fikar told me Faisal left the castle earlier," said Kareem. The PA's long face looked tired. There were deep brackets at the

23

sides of his mouth. With his dark suit and touch of gray at the temples, he looked like a high-powered executive, not someone who was in reality a glorified secretary.

"He's probably gone to Khaldun again," said Miftah in his gruff voice. "He's been going there quite often."

The meal proceeded pleasantly. Ghazala did most of the talking, with the other adults joining in. The only one who did not speak was Mrs. Haddad. The tutor had a distant expression on her face, as if her thoughts were miles away.

LATER, WHEN LAYLA returned to her suite, there came a knock at the door and the maid, Nura, entered.

"I'm here to refill your refrigerator," she said.

"Sure, go ahead."

Nura crouched down and began to replenish the boxes of juice and snacks with her small, slender fingers.

She's young and pretty but so serious.

"Nura, it must be a lot of work taking care of such a large castle."

"It is, but there are many of us to do it."

"Have you worked here a long time?"

"Yes, since I finished school four years ago." With a wistful look on her face, she said, "I would have loved to go to university, but after my father died, it was not financially possible."

"You have other family?"

Nura closed the refrigerator and stood up. "Yes. My mother and two sisters live in Khaldun."

"Do you like working here?"

A pinched look came over the maid's face. She said almost in a whisper, "I used to love it but now I hate it. Sometimes I feel like I'm in the middle of a dream and it will all go away when I wake up. But there's no escape for me."

There was such a ring of despair in the maid's voice that Layla stared at her in surprise.

"What do you mean?"

Fixing Layla with a fierce look, Nura said, "You shouldn't have come here. Evil things have happened. And more evil is to come. You should leave. Or there will be no escape from the evil."

Chapter Three
In the Garden of Dreams

"**W**HAT EVIL?"
NURA shook her head, her eyes wide and fearful. "I don't know myself. But it's around us, waiting and watching. I can feel it all the time. Leave, before it's too late."

Layla shivered as the maid walked out the door. Nura had sounded like an oracle of doom. *What evil could she be talking about? She had to be crazy in the head.*

As Layla lay in bed later, she could not push the maid's ominous warning out of her head. Her ears were cocked for the slightest sound and she almost jumped out of her skin when a tree branch scraped against the window. It sounded like phantom fingers trying to open it. She stared at the outline of the furniture in her room. *What menacing shapes they take on in the dark when one's imagination is working overtime.*

When she finally fell asleep, it was to dream she was being chased down the dark hallways of the castle by a shadowy figure.

THE NEXT MORNING, Layla told her brother and friends what the maid had told her.

"What evil could be going on here?" asked Adam. "We're in the middle of nowhere."

Zahra said, "She's probably a bit crazy."

"Yes, just ignore here," said Zaid.

Layla was more than happy to do so. After a long, leisurely breakfast, they decided to go exploring, starting with the forecourt. Bright sunlight streamed onto the gray tiles, reflecting off the windows of the vehicles and sending heat waves shimmering above. Daylight revealed in more detail what darkness had concealed on the night of their arrival. Beneath the portico, were low wooden benches for sitting.

Layla looked up at the castle. It did not look as creepy as it did at night. A tower rose at each end to embrace the sky while its dark, colossal façade seemed to take on a softer cast in the morning sunlight. The teenagers stopped a few moments to admire a blue Mercedes-Benz in the parking lot. The red Saab Layla had seen last night was not among the vehicles there.

They turned around when they heard a meow. An exotic silver-colored cat with black stripes and green eyes came slinking towards them. It stopped several feet away and stared at them with a disdainful look, its tail waving from side to side.

Layla walked over to it. "Hello, you wee little beastie. You're a beauty, aren't you?"

The cat hissed. At that moment, there came the low humming throb of an engine. Layla watched as the red Saab she had thought about earlier came speeding into the forecourt. Spooked by the sound, the cat ran across the path of the approaching vehicle and, like most animals were wont to do, stood frozen as the car came closer.

"Bilqis!" a voice cried in warning. "Bilqis!"

As Tariq came running across the forecourt, Layla, who stood closest to the cat, darted forward, grabbed the petrified animal, and dashed to the side. The Saab slowed down before proceeding to the parking lot. Faisal stepped out of the car and came up to them, a scowl on his face. He looked somewhat the worse for wear. His jeans and blue short-sleeved shirt were rumpled, and his hair mussed. Bleary eyes and a dark stubble on his chin completed his unkempt appearance.

Tariq rounded on him.

"How could you be so reckless?" he cried. "You almost ran over Layla and Bilqis."

"Oh, don't be so dramatic," snapped Faisal, his nostrils flaring. "And young lady," he turned a scathing glance on Layla, "it was foolish of you to jump in front of me like that."

"I'm sorry." Layla was still trembling inside with reaction. "I was afraid you'd run over the cat."

"That wild creature would have been no great loss, believe me," said Faisal before turning on his heels and stalking into the castle.

"Are you alright?" Tariq asked Layla. "You're not hurt, are you?"

"I'm fine. Just a bit shaken."

"Thank you for saving Bilqis." Tariq took the cat from Layla. "She's usually faster on her feet than what you saw."

"Tariq, why did Faisal call your cat a wild creature?" asked Zaid.

"Bilqis is not an ordinary domestic cat. She's half wildcat."

"She won't scratch me if I pet her, will she?" asked Zahra.

"*La.* No. Bilqis is not very friendly, but she's tame."

"She's as regal as her namesake, the Queen of Sheba," said Adam.

"She is, isn't she?" Tariq smiled for the first time since they met him. The smile erased the sadness from his face, giving them a glimpse of a carefree, teenage boy. Like Adam and Zaid, he was also attired in jeans and a T-shirt.

"How long have you had her?" asked Layla.

A bleak look came over Tariq's face. "A little before I came to live here three years ago. We lived in Rafah Province before my parents died. Bilqis's ancestors came from the mountains there. I really appreciate what you did. If there's any favor I can do in return, you must tell me."

Layla remembered Shaykh Sulaiman's words. "There's something I'd like to ask of you."

"What is it?"

"I'd like you to be friends with us and show us around."

"Of course, I can do that. I have lessons with Mrs. Haddad in the mornings from Monday to Thursday. I can show you around in the afternoons. Meet me in the domed hall at three this afternoon."

"We sure will," said Adam.

"Why are you still having lessons?" said Zahra. "Your grandfather told us you're going away to university soon."

"Yes, in mid-August, the day before you all leave to go home. It's been our family tradition to attend university in England. That's why Grandfather hired an English tutor for me and Hala. Mrs. Haddad's a bit strict but she's very educated. She'll be leaving when I do. She and Hala don't get along very well, so she didn't want to stay. We're making the most of the time we have left. I must go back to the classroom before she wonders why I'm taking such a long break. See you at three."

They watched as he and Bilqis walked across the forecourt and vanished through a door they had not even noticed before.

WHEN THEY MET with Tariq in the domed hall at three that afternoon, he took them on a tour inside the castle. There were five levels but only two were livable spaces. On the first floor was a huge kitchen, a servants' lounge, the dining areas, and the domed hall in the middle. Tucked next to the domed hall was a mosque. It had the same soaring ceiling as the rest of the castle, with a thick carpet and calligraphy on the walls. Shaded windows ensconced it in a cocoon of tranquility. The mosque could be accessed from inside the castle as well as from the forecourt.

At the other end of the first floor was Shaykh Sulaiman's suite and those of his nurse and PA. There was a large office on that side as well and the classroom where Mrs. Haddad did her teaching. On the second floor were the family suites. Tariq gave them a quick look inside his. It was much larger than the guest suites. In addition to the sitting room and bedchamber, he had a study room with a computer and bookshelves that were crammed with books.

"We're going to the recreation area next," he said, leading them back to the stairs.

On the first floor, he took them through the hallways to a back door that opened into a huge, square-shaped courtyard. Coming from the coolness inside the castle, the blast of heat was almost a shock. Layla shaded her eyes from the sun as she stared around. The courtyard was paved with beige ceramic tiles and lined with giant terra cotta urns of blooming flowers. Date palms and olive trees rimmed its circumference, their branches barely moving in the humid air. Scattered under the shade were wicker chairs here and there. Dominating the center of the courtyard was a gurgling, three-tiered stone fountain. On either side of the courtyard were more apartments.

Tariq said, "As you can see, the castle is u-shaped, with the main building in front and these two connecting ones at the back." Pointing to the wing on the left, he said, "Your suites are at the top there and can be reached from the main building. The recreation area is below." Pointing to the wing on the right, he said, "That wing also has guest suites at the top. The servant quarters are below. Most of the servants commute from Khaldun but some of them live in. At the back of the courtyard is the orchard." He pointed to a green wall of trees.

"We had no idea we were coming to a castle," said Layla as they stared around the charming courtyard.

"There's a few of them in the region. This one was built in the sixteenth century by the reigning Sultan of Ghassan. That was during the Ottoman period, so it's over five hundred years old. It was built of black basalt rocks. There have been some changes by other sultans but most of what you see is the original castle."

"I noticed there's a wall around it," said Adam.

"Yes, in the old days, it protected the castle. There were several postern or hidden gates that allowed the castle folk to come and go secretly. These days, there's no invading army to be afraid of. Just wild animals."

"Yes, we heard an animal screaming the first night we came," said Layla. "It was scary."

Something strange flashed across Tariq's face before he pointed to an arch-shaped entrance on the left. "That arcade leads into the *ghaf* grove. There are three of them total on that side. You can only get to the grove through them. As you can see, you're the only ones in this wing. You've got the *ghaf* grove to yourselves."

They came to a stop before wide cedar doors and Tariq said, "This is the recreation area."

It was a large space built with a series of high, narrow windows that gave glimpses of the green grove outside. Inside were ping pong and pool tables, and several game machines. In separate compartments were a small movie theater, a kidney-shaped swimming pool and a gym. The gym was equipped with a treadmill and other exercise machines.

Tariq said, "Qais, who's a physical therapist as well as a

nurse, brings Grandfather to the gym for therapy a few times a week. You might run into them occasionally."

"We should have a lot of fun here," said Adam, looking about him with interest.

"I'd love to use the swimming pool," said Zahra.

"Me too," said Layla, still feeling the heat from the courtyard.

Zaid held up a small, red bat. "I'd like to challenge you all to a game of ping pong sometime."

Adam gave a wolfish grin. "Only if you're ready for a good whupping."

"In your dreams," said Zaid.

"I'll take you to see the orchard now," said Tariq. "And a very special place at the back of it."

He took them across the courtyard toward the great wall of trees. At the end, a brick pathway lay before them, forking to the right and left. Tariq came to a stop and said, "The right pathway goes to the stables and the left pathway to an old *qasabah* or lookout tower. In the old days, the tower was used as a lookout point for enemies coming to lay siege on the castle."

"It looks very high," said Layla, catching sight of the old structure rising above the trees. *It would be an interesting place to explore another time.*

"Yes, it's very high," said Tariq, an odd note in his voice.

They continued forward under the cool haven of the trees. The pathway meandered in several directions. As they walked below the shady boughs, Tariq pointed out the different fruit trees to them. Along the way, they passed two gardeners hard at work, sweat streaming down their faces.

The trees gave way to a secluded garden encircled by towering cypresses and filled with flowers in beds of assorted shapes and sizes. Among them were clusters of shrubbery and arbors of red, pink and white roses. In the very center stood a rock fountain, its water dribbling rhythmically onto colored rocks at the base. Butterflies flitted among the flowers while a bee droned among the shrubbery. At the back, under the shade of the cypresses, were two white stone benches.

"Welcome to the Garden of Dreams," said Tariq.

"What a lovely garden," said Zahra, her eyes lighting up with pleasure.

Gesturing to the benches, Tariq said, "Come, let's sit here for a bit."

Though they sat in the shade, Layla could still feel the sharp warmth of the sun. She breathed in the fragrant aroma of jasmine and roses. "It's like a little paradise here. Who gave it that name?"

"My grandmother. She loved gardening. Once, she took a nap here and had some good dreams. Since then, she called it the Garden of Dreams."

"It sounds so poetic," murmured Zahra. "As if it's an enchanted garden."

"Grandfather used to come here often after Grandmother died. I guess it made him feel close to her even though she's gone. I pray every day that he continues to get stronger. I don't want to lose him yet. This is his second stroke. Dr. Hakam says Grandfather is not out of danger yet. I'm very worried."

"When did he have the first stroke?" asked Zaid.

"It was after my parents died. It took him almost a year to recover. During that time, I came to live here, and Kareem was hired as his PA."

"Does he have any more relatives besides the cousins?" asked Adam.

"Some very distant ones. The cousins are the closest blood relations."

"Have they lived here a long time?" asked Layla.

"Suha has been living here since she was eight. Aunt Ghazzy and Uncle Bilal have been here for the past six years. Faisal came the same time I did, three years ago. Uncle Miftah and Hala moved in after he and Suha got married two and a half years ago."

"The cousins don't seem to get along with each other," said Zaid.

"They're usually better behaved when Grandfather's around. One day he heard them arguing and threatened to reduce their bequests if they didn't make peace and get along with each other. Aunt Ghazzy often reminds them of this."

That's why they were afraid of his anger.

"Hala doesn't seem to get along with her stepmother either," said Zahra.

Tariq sighed. "She's been furious ever since Uncle Miftah and Suha got married."

"Suha seems so nice," said Zahra. "And she's not that old."

"Yes, she's the youngest of Grandfather's cousins. Her mother died when she was eight. Her father didn't have much time for her so Grandfather brought her to live here. She and Uncle Rashid are the same age. They grew up together and went to study in England at the same time. After they returned, there was talk about a match between them. Uncle Rashid wasn't in favor of it. He told me Suha was like a sister to him. After Miftah became widowed, she accepted his offer of marriage. Hala didn't get along with her from the start and still doesn't."

"Hala must find it hard to live here without friends of her own age," said Zaid.

"She didn't really mind because they used to travel a lot. Uncle Miftah and Suha love going on trips. Aunt Ghazzy and Uncle Bilal went away often too and as for Faisal, he was more often away than here. But since Grandfather became ill, they haven't gone anywhere except for short trips to Khaldun. That's why Hala's been acting up. She wants to go places and do things."

"Do the cousins do any kind of work?" said Adam.

"Yes, they work from here. Grandfather doesn't like idleness. Uncle Bilal is a freelance researcher and Aunt Ghazzy helps him. The others work for the Al-Khalili Corporation. Uncle Miftah and Suha are accountants and Faisal is an information technologist."

"Your grandfather mentioned an uncle when he visited our grandfather's house in Midan last year," said Layla. "The one who made a deathbed confession about the Moon of Masarrah."

"*Na'am.* Yes, that was Uncle Husam, Suha's father. He actually died just a few weeks before my parents. He had always been the black sheep of the family. After he confessed about the Moon, he also revealed he had gotten married to a *bedu* woman when he was twenty-two but left her six months later for a wealthy widow. The *bedu* woman had been pregnant at the time he left. Before he died, he begged Grandfather to find her and the child. After Grandfather recovered from his first stroke, he started the search for them before he went looking for the Moon. But they couldn't be found. More than forty years have gone by since then. Most of the *bedu* have become people of the cities now. Some have even migrated to other countries."

"So, Uncle Husam had a son or daughter he didn't even know about?" asked Zahra.

"I guess so. He or she would be half-brother or half-sister to Suha."

"What an age difference that would be," said Adam. "Suha is in her twenties and her half-brother or half-sister would be in their forties."

"Was Suha's mother the wealthy widow?" asked Layla.

"Oh, no. That marriage lasted just a few years. Suha is from his third wife, who he married years later."

"How long were your grandparents married?" asked Zaid. "And how many children did they have?"

"They were married for twenty-five years when Grandmother passed away. They had a son and a daughter, who have both passed away too. The son was my father, of course. Grandfather then remarried, and Uncle Rashid was born."

"So Rashid is really your half-uncle," said Adam.

"Yes. His mother passed away fifteen years after the marriage. And now, Uncle Rashid is gone too."

"Auntie Ghazala told us he died in the desert," said Layla, curious to know about the "circumstances" Ghazala had spoken about.

"Yes, he was on the Board of the Al-Khalili Corporation, but in his spare time, he was an honorary member of the Wildlife Conservation Society of Ghassan. He would often make trips to the Nawaf Desert to check that there was no illegal hunting of endangered species. One day he went and never came back. His horse returned alone in the evening. We knew then that something had happened. A search party went out at once to look for him. It was night and there was very little we could see. The next morning, we searched the desert but still couldn't find him."

"Oh, that must have been awful," said Zahra.

"Yes, it was terrible not knowing what had happened to him. There was only one place left to search and that was in Gurian Ravine. It's very deep and only rappellers, those who are experts at climbing down with ropes and special equipment, would be able to get down there. A rappelling team with a helicopter arrived that afternoon. They found Uncle Rashid's bloodstained shirt, rifle, and cell phone on the rocks at the bottom. He had liked climbing up the plateau to look for mountain lizards. The police thought he must have missed his footing and fallen to his death. And the hyenas and wolves living in the ravine must have dragged his body to their underground lairs. They gave a verdict of accidental death by falling."

"Oh my God, that's horrible," said Layla. "So that's what Auntie Ghazala meant when she said, 'because of the circumstances, his death wasn't publicized.'"

"Yes, if the media had learned of how Uncle Rashid died, they would have come to the castle like a pack of wolves. The rappellers and the staff who work here are the only people who know. They were sworn to secrecy. The last thing Grandfather wanted was for the media to play up all the gory details of Uncle Rashid's death. When he gets better and can deal with the sensation it will cause, he'll make the announcement then."

"What a terrible way for your uncle to die," said Adam. "One wrong move and that was the end."

"Yes, the police said he must have died instantly on the rocks below. The only problem is, I don't believe it was an accident."

"What do you mean?" asked Zaid.

"I think Uncle Rashid was murdered."

Chapter Four
The New Arrival

THEY ALL GAPED at Tariq.

"Why do you think that?" asked Zahra after they had recovered from the surprise.

"Because of what Uncle Rashid said to me a few days before he died. I was sick with bronchitis at the time. I had taken the medicine Dr. Hakam had prescribed when Uncle Rashid came to visit me. As he began telling me about the trip he had taken to Russia, I felt drowsy. My mind wandered as he spoke, and I don't remember what he told me. When he got up to leave, I remembered what he said then."

"What did he say?" asked Layla.

"He said, 'Tariq, I don't know who I can trust now but don't tell anyone what I've told you, okay? I'm going to find out who's behind it and put a stop to it, so don't worry.' When he died a few days later, his words took on a new meaning. That's when I began to believe his death might not have been an accident. I've tried to remember what else he told me, but I just can't."

"Maybe it will come back to you sometime," said Adam.

"I hope so."

"Did you tell anyone of your suspicion?" asked Zaid.

"No, I didn't. What could I have said? That I suspected Uncle Rashid had been murdered because of a conversation I don't even remember? I just couldn't add more to Grandfather's grief. Hearing something like that might have killed him outright. You must promise not to say anything to anyone."

"We promise," they all said.

"Thank you."

At that moment, they heard the crackling of twigs.

"Someone's coming," said Zahra.

When no one appeared in sight, Tariq said, "It was probably a jerboa."

"What's a jerboa?" asked Adam.

"It's a kangaroo rat," said Tariq. "They're quite common around deserts and oases."

"It sounded like someone walking over the twigs," said Zahra. "I guess I was wrong."

"Let's go back to the castle," said Tariq. "There's a place I want to show you in the forecourt."

When they returned to the castle, they found Bilqis wandering in the hallway. She gave a loud meow when she saw them.

"Is that an apology?" Tariq stooped and picked up the cat. "Are you in a better mood now?"

"Why, was she in a bad mood earlier?" asked Zahra.

"Yes, she was sulking under the bed and refused to come out when I called her."

Layla's mouth tilted up at the corners. "Sulking? I didn't know cats could sulk."

"Oh, this one does. She sits and glares and even tries to pout."

Zahra chuckled. "Why was she sulking?"

"I scolded her for scratching Mrs. Haddad this morning."

"You naughty kitty." Layla stroked the cat. "What sharp claws you have."

"All the better to scratch you with," said Adam in a gruff voice.

Zahra began stroking the cat too. Bilqis arched her back, purring in pleasure as she nuzzled against their fingers.

Tariq smiled. "She really likes you all. Usually it takes her a while to warm up to people. She positively loathes Mrs. Haddad. Although I think the feeling is mutual."

"She must not like tutors," said Layla.

The smile left Tariq's face. "No, she was fond of my previous tutor." Changing the subject abruptly, he asked, "Can you all ride?"

Zaid said, "Yes, Zahra and I learned when we were living in England."

"Adam and I have taken some lessons," said Layla, "but we could do with a bit more practice."

"We sure can," Adam agreed. "We haven't had a lesson in months."

"You can have some while you're here," said Tariq. "I'll take you over to the stables this evening to meet Hatem. He's the head groom there and will help choose suitable horses for you. Since tomorrow is Friday and I'm free the entire day, I'll give you a tour of the stables in the morning and we'll begin riding lessons in the mid-afternoon when the sun's not so fierce. Now, let's go to the forecourt."

In the forecourt, Faisal's Saab was still there as well as the blue Mercedes-Benz they had admired earlier.

"Those are some cool wheels," said Zaid. "Who does the Mercedes-Benz belong to?"

"You like it?" asked Tariq. "It's mine."

"Awesome," said Adam. "You must take us for a ride in it one day."

Tariq smiled. "I will, *insha Allah*. Come, let me show you the caravanserai now."

"Caravanserai?" said Layla. "What's that?"

"It's a part of the castle that was used in the old days to shelter travelers and their caravans of goods. It had baths and sleeping chambers and even pens for the animals."

The caravanserai was at the rightmost end of the castle and had its own courtyard. Like all relics from bygone eras, it had an empty, forlorn look. Layla could just imagine the flurry of activities that took place in the old days when a caravan pulled in.

"You've now finished your tour of the renowned Dukhan Castle," said Tariq. "Feel free to explore further if you wish."

"How did the castle and oasis get its name?" asked Zahra.

"*Ta'al*. Come, I'll show you," said Tariq.

They followed him across the forecourt and through the gate. It swung open automatically to let them through. They walked out to the road. Surrounding them were limestone hills strewn with small stones and sprouting hardy green shrubs. When they came to an elevation in the road, Tariq stopped.

Turning towards the castle, he pointed and said, "Look behind the castle now. What do you see?"

The castle was covered in afternoon sunlight. The teenagers shaded their eyes and squinted upwards. In the distance, they saw a dark range of hills, their jagged peaks seeming to disappear into the clouds.

"I see hills," said Zaid.

"Yes, that's the Dukhan Hills," said Tariq. "The clouds make them appear as if they're covered in smoke. That's how the name came about."

Adam pointed to the tall, dark structure at the back of the castle. "Tariq, is that the lookout tower?"

"Yes, it is. The castle is the only building for miles around. The nearest city is Khaldun. It's an hour away."

"Is Khaldun as large as Ghassan City?" asked Zahra.

"No. Neither is it as modern. Suha and Hala prefer to shop in Ghassan City. They like the malls there."

"Adam and I are hoping we can take a trip there when our parents come," said Layla. "We'd love to see Ghassan City."

"It's a special city," said Tariq. "Of the three cities we have, it's the only one next to the sea."

When they returned to the forecourt, Layla remembered the woman in white she had seen on the night of their arrival.

"Tariq, on the night we came, I saw a woman wearing allover white, looking out from one of the windows. I've seen the maids wearing allover black, but I haven't seen anyone wearing white like that. Who could it have been?"

A startled look flashed across Tariq's face and he stared up at the windows with an uneasy expression. As Layla wondered at Tariq's odd reaction, they heard the soft purr of an engine. A gray Mitsubishi Outlander came gliding into the forecourt. At the wheel was a woman in *hijab*.

Tariq's face lit up. "It's Jumana. She's here at last."

The mysterious Jumana is finally here.

"Who is she?" asked Layla.

"Her father is the Governor of Tarub Province and is Grandfather's dear friend. Jum-Jum was engaged to Uncle Rashid and their wedding was to have been at the end of June. She would have visited sooner but she became ill after Uncle Rashid's death."

The Mitsubishi came to a stop in the parking lot. They watched as a petite woman stepped out and walked with short, graceful steps towards them. Clad in a plain black gown and a paisley-patterned gray scarf, she was simply dressed. But she was one of the most beautiful women Layla had ever seen. She was about twenty-four, with a delicate diamond-shaped face, wide amber eyes and a creamy complexion.

After introductions were over, she said in a low, lilting voice, "I'm pleased to meet you. I hope you enjoy your stay here."

The teenagers joined the family in the domed hall to partake of the refreshments in honor of Jumana's arrival. Two large trolleys piled with beverages, sandwiches, and confectionery had been brought in.

"It's hard to believe Rashid is gone." Ghazala picked up a piece of pistachio cake. "It must be difficult coming back here, Jumana."

"It is, Ghazzy." Jumana took a sip from a cup of tea.

She's still wearing a diamond engagement ring.

"I think you're very brave." Suha spread hummus on a piece of bread with long, well-manicured fingers. "I don't think I'd have been able to come back so soon."

"I'm glad you came, Jum-Jum," said Hala. Her wide lips were turned up in a smile. It was a change from its usual petulant droop. "You can't imagine how dull it's been with Uncle Sulaiman ill and everyone walking around with long faces. If not for Tariq, I would have gone crazy." She smiled at the youth, who gave her a smile in return.

"Poor Sulaiman is devastated." Miftah took a bite of his sandwich. "It was a great blow to lose his only remaining offspring."

"I've been so worried about him," said Jumana. "Is he doing any better?"

"A little," said Tariq. "He'll be very happy to see you."

Faisal was leaning back on the couch, staring up at the chandelier as if it held more interest than the conversation. After nearly running down Tariq's pet that morning, he must have gotten a good rest after lunch. He looked his suave self again, clean-shaven and not a hair out of place.

Removing his eyes from the ceiling, he said, "Maybe Jumana can set Sulaiman's mind at rest about that nasty bit of gossip going around the castle. He was very distressed when he heard it."

"Gossip?" asked Jumana, her eyes wide. "What do you mean?"

Yes, what gossip?

There was an awkward silence. Jumana looked from one cousin to the next, a frown puckering her brow.

"It's just idle servants wagging their tongues," said Ghazala, glaring at Faisal. "It's nothing to worry about."

Faisal shrugged. "Jumana will hear of it sooner or later. You can't keep anything a secret around here."

"Why don't you tell me what it is?" said Jumana, giving him a steely look.

"Fine. The servants were saying that you and Rashid had an argument on your last visit here. A few days before he died."

Chapter Five
The Lookout Tower

COLOR FLARED IN Jumana's face and then fled, leaving her ashen. Her slender fingers gripped the teacup tightly. The next moment, her chin rose. Setting the teacup carefully on the coffee table, she stood up. "I've never paid attention to gossip and rumors before and I won't start now. If you'll excuse me, I'm rather tired and would like to go to my room."

After she left, Ghazala turned angrily to Faisal. "Really, Faisal. You don't have a considerate bone in your body. You didn't even let Jumana finish her tea before you opened your mouth and upset her."

Faisal looked unrepentant. "She's a big girl. She can handle it."

Suha said, "I agree that Faisal's timing could have been better, Ghazzy, but he's right. Jumana would have found out sooner or later."

"It should have been later," said Miftah. "There was no need to tell her as soon as she arrived. It was ill-mannered."

"You're all a bunch of cowards," said Faisal, striding out of the domed hall in a huff.

The rest of the family followed, leaving Tariq and the teenagers alone there.

Tariq sighed. "Poor Jumana. What a welcome. Let's go over to the stables now. I want to catch Hatem before he leaves."

As they entered the inner courtyard, Layla's curiosity got the better of her. "Tariq, is it true what Faisal said? Did your uncle and Jumana have an argument a few days before he died?"

"I'm not sure. Remember, I was ill at the time. Hala was the one who told me about it. She'd heard the adults talking about it. According to the servants, Uncle Rashid and Jum-Jum met in the courtyard and began talking. From the expressions on their faces and their hand gestures, it looked like they were having an argument. They both looked upset afterwards and Jum-Jum left the next day when she was supposed to have stayed out the week. She didn't even come to say goodbye to me. That's unlike her. I guess we'll never know what happened unless she breaks her silence."

At the edge of the courtyard, they followed the red brick pathway on the right. They walked for several minutes until they came to the low line of buildings which housed the stables and an office. All was quiet, as work had finished for the day. They found Hatem in the office.

The head groom was a tall, broad-shouldered man in his late twenties, with close-cropped hair and a neat beard. A long, thin scar slashed across the right side of his face from cheekbone to jaw, giving him a sinister appearance. He was dressed in a uniform of baggy black pants and black short-sleeved shirt with brass buttons. After Tariq performed the introductions and explained the purpose of their visit, Hatem studied them, his eyes measuring their sizes for the horses.

"We have several horses which will be suitable," he said. "They'll be ready for you tomorrow."

"Thank you, Hatem," said Tariq. "Have a good night. We'll see you tomorrow."

After they were out of earshot, Zahra said, "What a scary looking man. How did he get that scar on his face?"

"I don't think he's ever told anyone," said Tariq. "He's wonderful with the horses and that's what matters."

When they came to the fork again, Layla glanced up at the lookout tower. "Tariq, can we take a quick look at the tower? It looks very interesting."

Tariq seemed oddly hesitant as he stared up at the hulking structure. Finally, he said, "Yes, of course. Let's go."

They followed him down the tree-lined path which curved deeply to the right before ending in a clearing. The solitary tower loomed in the late afternoon light, standing about seven stories tall. It seemed solid and sturdy but had a gothic, forsaken air about it. Built of the same black basalt rocks as the castle, there were bits of green moss clinging between the cracks and thick, black vines twining their way to the top. To Layla, the vines seemed like skeletal arms slowly suffocating the tower. She gave a sudden shiver. The vibe she was getting here was not good.

"Goodness, that tower sure looks creepy." Adam craned his neck to get a better view.

"It doesn't have a pleasant history," said Tariq. "Legend has it that a guard was found poisoned there, another broke his neck falling down the stairs, and a female servant was found strangled. And last December, my previous tutor jumped to her death from the window."

The teenagers stared in shock at Tariq.

"Oh my God, that's awful," said Layla.

"Horrible." Zahra shuddered.

Adam's eyes moved from window to ground. "That's a really long way to fall."

"Yes, she must have died instantly," said Zaid.

"Why did she do it?" asked Layla.

"I'll tell you when we get up there. It's not a pleasant story."

The base of the tower was a large, circular space which held a long, spiral stairway made of stone. After hearing of the guard falling to his death, the teenagers took extra care to hold on to the handrails as they climbed. The twisting, hollow cavity of the stairway would have been dark if not for bits of daylight coming through slits in the wall shaft. At last, they reached the top of the stairs.

They were standing on a narrow, rectangular landing with a battered wooden door facing them. Tariq opened the door and they entered a spacious, round chamber with wooden floors and a vaulted ceiling. The walls were plastered with glazed stone tiles and rectangular peepholes were carved out at standing height. To the right were two chairs encircling a small table and to the left, an ancient brick fireplace with a wooden rocking chair next to it. Facing them across the floor was a single window.

Tariq gestured to the window. "As you can see, Grandfather had the window boarded up. He didn't want any tragedies like that ever happening again."

They stared at the window from where the horrendous act had taken place. It was tall, wide and arch-shaped at the top. Thick bars of wood had been nailed across the bottom, leaving just a strip of glass free above. The light coming through was sparse, filling the room with murky shadows.

"Take a look through the peepholes before it gets too dark," said Tariq. "The view is spectacular."

The view was indeed spectacular as they peered out. From the great height of the tower, the countryside yielded all its secrets. They saw the dark outline of the Dukhan Hills, the many limestone hills and the vast emptiness of the terrain around them. In the old days, no enemy approaching the castle would have remained undetected by the guards keeping watch.

A sweet odor hung in the air, tickling their noses.

Zaid sniffed. "It smells like incense. Someone must have lit an incense stick."

"That's strange," said Tariq. "I didn't think anyone would want to come up here after what happened."

"Tell us about it," said Adam.

"Let's sit," said Tariq. "We'll get tired standing up."

The girls sat on the chairs while Zaid took the rocking chair. Adam and Tariq sat on the floor, their backs against the wall.

Tariq said, "My tutor's name was Lamis. She was hired last July by Grandfather. Like Mrs. Haddad, she was from England but much younger. She had settled in and we were doing quite well. Then Uncle Rashid and Jum-Jum announced their engagement at the end of December. That's when the nightmare began."

"What happened?" said Layla.

"Grandfather held an engagement dinner for them. As an engagement gift, Uncle Rashid gave Jum-Jum an antique pearl bracelet that had belonged to his mother. By lunch the next day, she discovered it was missing from her room. Someone had stolen it. Uncle Rashid was very upset. He wanted to bring in the police but Jum-Jum told him to wait. She said whoever stole the bracelet might return it once they realized they would get into trouble. The next day passed without the bracelet being returned. The morning after that, Lamis's body was found at the foot of the tower. On this very table," Tariq pointed, "she left a letter saying she had stolen the bracelet and was ending her life because Uncle Rashid had broken his promise to marry her."

"Did he really?" said Layla.

"Of course not." Tariq's voice was indignant. "He never had eyes for anyone else but Jum-Jum. He was a very eligible bachelor, but he waited until she finished her studies abroad before proposing to her. The suicide and letter were great shocks to everyone. Especially for Uncle Rashid and Jum-Jum. The police, knowing of no other reason why Lamis would kill herself, believed what she claimed in the letter even though Uncle Rashid denied it as false. Tongues started to wag and the newspapers in Khaldun had a field day with it, calling Uncle Rashid all sorts of nasty names. That's why Grandfather was determined to keep Uncle Rashid's death out of the news. They would have dug up the whole story of Lamis's suicide again."

"Was the bracelet ever found?" asked Zahra.

"No, it wasn't."

"Your tutor's family must have been shocked," said Zaid.

"It took a while to find them in England since she gave no contact information. Grandfather took care of the burial arrangements and when her family was finally located, he explained what had happened and offered them financial compensation since she died in our employment. At the end of January, he hired Mrs. Haddad to replace her. Things had settled back to almost normal when something weird happened in March."

"What do you mean by weird?" said Adam.

"A maid went into hysterics one night. She said she heard a bloodcurdling scream and saw a woman dressed all in white standing by the orchard."

Chapter Six

Voices in the Dark

"THE WOMAN IN White," Layla exclaimed. "That's who I must have seen the night we came. I remember thinking that if ghosts were real, she'd definitely be one. And it must have been her screaming in the *ghaf* grove. Oh my goodness, this is so creepy."

"I thought it must have been her when you said you'd heard an animal screaming," said Tariq. "Only the servants have seen her and heard her so far. Sometimes they see her by the orchard or the arcades leading to the grove. No one's seen her inside the castle. I'm surprised you did."

"Maybe she wanted to give us a special welcome," said Adam.

"She can't be a real ghost, of course," said Zaid. "So who could she be?"

"We don't know," said Tariq. "No one's been able to catch her. After she was first seen, the servants secretly brought in an old woman from Khaldun who sells amulets. The old woman told them Lamis had become a *ghul* and is haunting the castle. After Uncle Rashid died, the old woman must have found out about it from one of the servants, even though they denied it. She came a few days later with more amulets. She told the servants that Lamis's *ghul* had sent Uncle Rashid to his death in the desert and ate his corpse in revenge. She said the *ghul* would not rest until all the men in the castle had gone to their doom, and Grandfather would be next. She's been banned from coming here again."

"Wow, I didn't know people here believe in such things as ghouls," said Layla. "I thought only people in the west did."

"Dad told us that the people in the west actually got their belief in ghouls from old Arabian folklores," said Zaid. "It happened after the stories of *The Thousand and One Nights* were translated into *The Arabian Nights*. The stories are full of *jinns*. A *ghul* was a *jinn* that walked the desert in the form of a beautiful woman. She would lure lustful men to their doom and eat their flesh. In the west, the *ghul* eventually became known as a ghoul, an evil spirit who robs graves and feeds on dead bodies."

Layla grimaced. "People have colorful imaginations."

"We know the *jinn* are shape shifters and can take different forms," said Zaid, "but I doubt the Woman in White is a real *ghul*."

"Try telling the servants that," said Tariq. "Some of them are very superstitious."

"Maybe that's what Nura was warning me about," said Layla.

Seeing Tariq's inquiring expression, she told him about the maid's warning.

"She had no business trying to scare you," said Tariq. "Grandfather will be angry if he hears about it."

"It's alright," said Layla. "She hasn't said anything to me again. But this Woman in White masquerade is weird. Why would anyone pretend to be a ghoul?"

"We haven't the faintest idea," said Tariq. "Let me know if you hear her again."

"I doubt she'll bother us again," said Adam.

AFTER THE DRAMA of Jumana's arrival, dinner turned out to be surprisingly pleasant.

Along with the family, Kareem, Mrs. Haddad, and the guests, it was quite a large gathering. Fourteen chairs were now occupied. Layla, wearing a brown floral dress with a solid brown scarf, was enjoying the meal. There was tangy baked chicken with flavored rice, marinated lamb *kebabs* and chicken *kofta* with bell peppers and onions. Conversation flowed as everyone ate.

Ghazala raised a glass of water to her lips, her emerald ring flashing in the light of the chandelier. She was wearing a midnight blue *abaya*. The style in which she tied her light-blue scarf made her bird-like features look softer. "How was your visit with Sulaiman, Jumana?"

"It was very emotional, Ghazzy," said Jumana. She was dressed in a peach *jilbab* with matching scarf. The ensemble brought out the creamy tone of her skin and the amber glow of her eyes. "He wept like a heartbroken child when he saw me. It's sad to see him like that. When I told him I would be spending a week, he insisted I stay until Tariq leaves. I couldn't refuse him. I don't have anything else of importance to do until school re-opens."

"You plan to continue teaching?" asked Suha. Hala's stepmother wore a deep-purple gown with batwing sleeves. Her light-purple scarf was pinned with the diamond pin she had worn the previous evening. Eyeshadow the same color as her gown accentuated her long lashes.

A fleeting look of sorrow flashed across Jumana's face. "Yes, I am. I thought I would be starting a new chapter in my life, but it wasn't meant to be."

"I'm sure your students will be happy to have you back," said Tariq.

The youth was dressed in a tan robe with embroidered cuffs. His curly hair was slicked back in an attractive style, emphasizing his chiseled features. He sat facing Layla, and soon engaged her and Adam in conversation. He was curious about their life in America and peppered them with many questions. Some of them were so funny that Layla laughed several times, the dimples in her cheeks flashing prettily.

She saw Hala watching her. There was a sullen twist to the other girl's lips. She wore a short-sleeved ivory dress, her frizzy hair in a coiffure with a matching headband. Her *kohl*-darkened eyes and pink lip gloss gave her a grown-up look.

As Ghazala's husband, Bilal, tore into a piece of chicken, Layla noticed that his upper canines were pointed, looking almost like fangs. *He looks like an owl and has the owl's habit of coming out at night. But he could just as well be a vampire with those pointed teeth.*

They were having dessert when the PA said, "By the way, I heard in Khaldun this morning that the Hooded Horseman was back."

"Really?" said Ghazala. "I thought he disappeared for good two years ago."

"He's been seen quite recently from what I hear," said Kareem.

"He was considered quite a hero for helping people in trouble, wasn't he?" asked Jumana.

"A lot of those stories were exaggerated," said Suha. "People love to embellish things."

Miftah nodded at his wife's remark. "Yes, that's true. Before he disappeared, there were stories about him killing someone."

"So, he wasn't quite the knight in shining armor on his trusty steed," said Faisal. "How disappointing."

"This Hooded Horseman seems to be quite a person of mystery," said Mrs. Haddad. "It could very well be the Hooded

Horsewoman. After all, who would know what lies beneath the hood?"

Layla looked in surprise at the tutor. Mrs. Haddad's manner had been quite aloof since dinner began. It was as if she sat on a lofty height, looking down with disdain upon the foibles of her fellow mortals. Her hair was up in its usual chignon and she was dressed in a green silk dress. It made her skin look sallow and her face even more gaunt.

"It cannot be a woman," said Bilal. He blinked bashfully behind his glasses as all eyes turned to him. "I saw him once on the outskirts of Khaldun. He seemed big and tall."

"Why Bilal," said Faisal, his hazel eyes filled with mischief, "was he coming to rescue you from the clutches of Ghazzy?"

Hala giggled and everyone else smiled in amusement.

Ghazala's pointed nose rose in the air. "Don't be childish, Faisal. You're an adult. Act like one."

"Your words have wounded me, Ghazzy." Faisal clutched at his chest. "Oh, how cruel you are."

Ghazala narrowed her eyes and held up her fork. "I'll give you another wound if you don't stop this nonsense."

Faisal grinned and Layla thought how charming he could be when he made the effort.

After the meal ended and everyone stood up to leave, Layla felt one of the pins in her scarf come loose.

"Go ahead," she said to the others. "I'll just run across to the bathroom and fix my scarf."

When she came out, she was surprised to see Hala standing outside. Layla smiled at her and gestured to the bathroom. "It's all yours."

There was no answering smile on Hala's face. Instead, she grabbed Layla's arm and hissed, "You think you're smart, don't you?"

"What do you mean?" Layla looked at her in surprise.

"Don't pretend you don't know what I'm talking about." Hala's voice was scornful. "You were flirting with Tariq during dinner. Trying to dazzle him with your loose American ways. You heard he's going to be a billionaire when Uncle Sulaiman dies, didn't you? Well, don't get any ideas because he was being friendly. He'll never marry a foreigner."

Layla looked at Hala with incredulous eyes. "I have no idea what you're talking about."

"You can stop the innocent act," said Hala. "Let me make it clear. Tariq's going to marry me in a few years, so keep your big eyes away from him."

As Hala flounced away, Layla stared after her in shock. She had no idea the girl had romantic feelings for Tariq. And she was aghast at what Hala had accused her of. Flirting? That conjured up images of girls and boys making eyes at each other and telling each other silly things. She had done neither of those things. How dare Hala accuse her of that?

When she returned upstairs, she told Zahra what had happened.

Zahra gaped at her friend. "She said what?"

"Exactly. Can you believe it?"

"Oh my, she's jealous of you."

"But why?"

Zahra grinned, her dark eyes dancing. She was wearing a salmon-colored ensemble this evening that brought out the golden-honey tone of her skin. "She's obviously set her sights on marrying Tariq and is afraid you'll steal him away. If my future husband paid me no attention during dinner and looked like he enjoyed talking to you, I'd be jealous too."

"He was talking to both me and Adam," said Layla, blushing a little. "Hala must be crazy to think I'm planning to steal him away or something. I'm only fourteen, for crying out loud. I don't plan to marry for years yet. I've never heard anything so ridiculous in my life."

"I don't think Tariq has a clue how Hala feels about him," said Zahra. "She's all gooey-eyed over him but he treats her like a younger sister. Men can be so blind about these things."

Layla chuckled. "You sound like a wise old woman. Yes, I'm sure Tariq has no idea the little witch wants to marry him. Maybe she plans to drag him kicking and screaming to the wedding."

Grinning impishly, Zahra said, "Tariq's kind of cute, isn't he? I think he likes your green eyes."

Layla rolled those green eyes at her friend. "Zahra Alkurdi, hold your tongue. I'm not ready to have a crush yet. And certainly not on a desert type like Tariq. He'll want his wife to stay home and have babies."

Zahra tut-tutted. "Layla Horani, I'm shocked at the words coming out of your mouth. Don't stereotype Tariq. And what's wrong with staying home and having babies? I wouldn't mind doing that."

"If you want to, it's fine. But I want to be a doctor like my Dad. And I'm going to marry someone who'll support me with that, *insha Allah.*"

"I want a career that will allow me to be at home with my babies. How about that?"

Layla's dimples came out again. "I like the way you think, sister. Oh, there's just one more thing."

"What?"

"I'll cut your tongue and feed it to the fishes if you tell the boys what Hala said."

WHEN LAYLA WENT to bed that night, she found it hard to fall asleep. She kept thinking about the confrontation with Hala and how downright mean the other girl had been. It was an unpleasant new experience being at the receiving end of someone's jealousy. The more Layla thought about it, the more restless she became. She had turned off the air conditioning because it had gotten too cold. Now she felt a bit warm. Perhaps if she opened the window, a bit of breeze might blow in and lull her to sleep.

Throwing off the covers, she went to the window and pulled the drapes aside. The air was thick with the scent of foliage. The moon had risen a bit and she stared out at the darkened trees as she listened to the hum of the night insects. *The view from my window would have been a lovely one if it had not been blocked by the ghafs.*

Hearing a rustling sound, Layla peered through the window screen at the ground below. She glimpsed a figure in a voluminous dark cloak. Moments later, the figure was swallowed up by the darkness. Who had it been? It seemed strange that anyone would be walking in the grove at night. Feeling sleepy now, she went back to bed, pulled the covers over her and quickly fell asleep.

Layla was not sure what woke her up later. It might have been the creaking limbs of the *ghaf* or the breeze drifting through the open window, causing the drapes to flutter noisily. Sliding off the bed, she went over to the window. The moon had risen higher and its light stole through the limbs of the *ghaf,* casting slithering shadows on the ground below. As she was about to close the window, Layla was startled to hear the faint murmur of voices. Her little bedside clock told her it was nearly twelve. Who could be in the grove at this hour?

From the sound of the voices, she could tell it was a man and a woman. They spoke in hushed tones and at one point, it seemed like they were having a heated argument. She heard a word here and there though it did not make sense to her. An owl began to hoot in the distance, drowning out the voices. After the hoots died away, there was silence once more in the grove.

Layla wondered who the man and woman could have been. Somehow, the whole episode struck her as sinister. She gave a slight shiver as she remembered the maid's warning — "Evil things have happened here. And more evil is to come. It's around us waiting and watching."

Closing the window, she returned to bed and huddled under the covers. *Just great. I'm getting spooked by the hired help now.*

Layla was destined to be disturbed for a second time that night. She had just dropped off to sleep when she was awakened by a scream. It was a keening of terrible torment that dragged her from the depths of slumber and had her cowering against the pillows in a panic.

Chapter Seven
Riding Lessons

T HE WOMAN IN *White. She's here again.*
As the lamentation died away and the night became
silent again, Layla's fear waned, and she fell back against
the pillows. What a horrible scream it had been. And it had
sounded so near. Like the Woman in White was just outside the
window. *But why is she trying to scare us? Is something really evil
going on here? Are we in danger?*

As Layla's heartbeat accelerated, she told herself to stop this
madness. The Woman in White was a big, fat fraud. She could
not do anything beyond scaring them. To calm her nerves, Layla
recited a short chapter from the *Qur'an* she had learnt as a little
girl. *Say, I seek refuge with Allah, The Lord of mankind, The King
of mankind, The God of mankind, from the evil of the whisperer,
who whispers in the breasts of mankind, from among the jinn and
mankind.*

Just before she fell asleep again, a thought hovered on the
periphery of Layla's mind, only to fade away like mist in the sun
as she finally slept.

"THE WOMAN IN White screamed again in the grove last night," said Zaid the next morning as they left the *ghaf* suites. He wore khaki slacks with a black cotton shirt and smelled faintly of *oud*. "Did you all hear her too?"

"Oh, yes," said Layla. "You'd have to be dead to the world not to have heard her."

"I guess we're the only ones who heard her since no one else sleeps in this wing," said Adam, running a hand over his hair. He had attempted to tame it with a little gel this morning.

"I hope she doesn't come again," said Zahra. "That scream was awful."

"You know what we should do if she comes again?" said Adam. "We should use the fire escape to go into the grove and catch her."

"Good idea," said Zaid. "Wouldn't it be great if we caught her?"

"Yes, I'd love to find out who our fake ghoul is." Layla's eyes shone with excitement. She went on to tell them about the figure in the dark cloak and the man and woman she had heard arguing.

"It's weird that people would be there at night," said Zahra.

"It could be normal behavior around here,'" said Adam. "I won't be surprised if someone comes dancing at dawn next."

Layla giggled. "Now, that would be a sight to see."

TARIQ TOOK THEM on the promised tour of the stables after breakfast. The sight of the horses - beautiful Arabians of noble lineage and graceful lines - would have gladdened the heart of any equestrian. They looked well-fed and well-cared for. Layla was not surprised when Tariq told them horses from the Al-Khalili stables were very much in demand by horse lovers and jockeys around the world. She watched in fascination as they snorted and stomped on the ground, swishing their tails from side to side to chase away flies. Layla had always loved being around horses and quite enjoyed the riding lessons she and Adam had started when they were younger.

While they watched the horses, Zaid told Tariq about the Woman in White screaming in the grove again last night.

"I can't believe she came there again," said Tariq. Wearing navy twill pants and a light-blue T-shirt he looked like a teenager from the west.

"If she comes again, we're planning to use the fire stairs to catch her," said Adam. "But we don't want anyone to know. If our ghoul hears of it, she'll be on the alert."

"I won't tell anyone," Tariq promised. "If I see her, I'll chase her down myself."

Layla said, "Earlier last night in the grove, I also saw a figure in a dark cloak and heard a man and woman arguing. It was before the Woman in White came screaming."

"It was probably the servants," said Tariq. "If they show up again, let me know. I'll tell Dhul Fikar to give them a warning."

Tariq hailed one of the passing grooms, a lean brown-skinned Indian man in his early twenties. The groom was wearing the same uniform of baggy black pants and short-sleeved black shirt with brass buttons that Hatem, the head groom, had worn last evening.

"Hello Raj, have the horses for our guests been chosen yet?"

Raj gave them a quick, curious look out of expressive black eyes before replying in halting Arabic, "Yes, Mr. Tariq. Mr. Hatem has them all picked out. They'll be saddled and waiting for you this afternoon."

"Thanks, Raj," said Tariq. "We'll see you later."

After leaving the stables, Tariq took them on the alternate route that led to the forecourt. The path curved around the right side of the castle, past an herb and vegetable garden that assailed them with a blend of aromas. When they passed by the kitchen courtyard, they smelled food and heard the drone of voices and the banging of utensils. Preparations for lunch were in full swing.

After passing by the sunroom and dining room, they turned into the forecourt, went past the caravanserai and returned inside the castle via the front door. They parted ways with Tariq as they went up to their suites to prepare for lunch and the Friday congregational prayer.

LATER, THE ENTIRE castle, including household, guests and employees, gathered in the mosque for the *Jumu'ah* prayer. Shaykh Sulaiman was brought in on a wheelchair by his nurse, Qais, who looked as if he could lift both the shaykh and his wheelchair without breaking a sweat. Everyone fussed around the patient and he smiled at the attention, though he still looked frail and spoke with the same slurred speech.

An imam from Khaldun delivered a stirring sermon on the story of Jacob who had prayed for patience when faced with the loss of his son, Joseph. Layla blinked tears away. The sermon couldn't be more apt. Joseph's brothers had told their father his beloved son had been devoured by a wild animal. Now, in a different place and a different time, another father had been told his son had suffered the same fate.

THAT AFTERNOON, THEY donned comfortable riding clothes and footwear before heading to the stables. The groom, Raj, took them to a shed and handed them riding helmets to wear. They followed him to the paddock where they found their mounts saddled and waiting. Layla and Adam were paired with placid mares named Ayah and Izza. Ayah was a gray color that seemed almost white, while Izza was the more common bay color. Zaid and Zahra, being more experienced riders, were matched with Dirar and Bandar, chestnut stallions foaled from the same mare. They all gazed in admiration at Jasim, Tariq's high-spirited ebony stallion.

"He's beautiful, isn't he?" Tariq's voice was proud. "He's of pure Najd blood."

With the aid of a mounting block, they seated themselves on their horses. Layla adjusted herself in the saddle, digging her feet in the stirrups and taking hold of Ayah's reins. She squeezed her legs lightly around the horse, cuing her to move. Under Tariq's guidance, they walked the horses around until they got accustomed to the feel of the animals and felt comfortable enough to move on to a slow trot. After trotting around for an hour, Tariq called a halt.

"That's it for today. I don't want to tire you too much. Once you put in enough practice, I'll take you to the fields outside. It's through that gate." He pointed to a wide gate in the wall.

As that moment, two riders came through the gate. It was Jumana and Hala. Layla admired the confident way Jumana handled her horse. She seemed to be an excellent equestrienne. Hala sat well on her horse too and looked to be an expert rider.

Jumana trotted over to them. She was wearing a bisque colored scarf, baggy khaki pants and a brown tunic. With her unique amber eyes and face aglow from her recent ride, she was the picture of vibrant femininity. After a moment's hesitation, Hala followed too. The girl was wearing a black track suit with yellow stripes. There was a healthy color in her cheeks and she seemed in better spirits.

"How are the riding lessons going?" said Jumana.

"Very well, thank you," Adam and Layla replied in unison.

"The more practice you put in, the better it gets," she said in her lilting voice. "But you've probably been told that umpteen times."

"Yes, we'll have to go to the riding school more often when we get back home," said Layla. "You look like you were born in the saddle."

Jumana gave a modest shrug. "I began learning to ride at the age of four. I've spent many hours in the saddle. You seem comfortable on your horses. That makes a big difference."

"Izza is a nice docile mare." Adam patted his horse. "It will be a while before I can handle a big brute like Jasim."

"I'm pleased with their progress," said Tariq. "I think they'll be ready for the fields soon."

"Yay," Layla cheered, her dimples flashing as she laughed. Tariq smiled at her exuberance and Layla's laughter faded as she saw the hard glint in Hala's eyes.

FAISAL WAS ABSENT again at dinner that evening.

"I don't see why he has to disappear without a word," said Ghazala. "We probably won't be able to get hold of him if Sulaiman should take a turn for the worse."

Sitting at her side, Bilal nodded in agreement at his wife's remark.

"You'll have no problem reaching Suha and I in Ghassan City," said Miftah. "We're going tomorrow and coming back on Monday evening. Hala really wants to see her uncle."

There was a smug expression on Hala's face.

She must be happy to finally get her way.

"We're still worried about Sulaiman," said Suha. "He's not out of danger yet."

"We hope he'll be fine while we're gone," said Miftah. "Should he have a relapse, call us right away."

"You all act as if the Shaykh is at death's door," said Mrs. Haddad. "I think it will take more than a stroke to topple the old man. He'll probably live a lot longer than any of you expect."

There was such a queer edge to the tutor's voice that Layla glanced sideways at her. Mrs. Haddad was leaning back in her chair, a strange twist to her lips. Her hair was pulled back in the severe bun she favored and she looked washed out in a button-down, off-white linen dress.

Ghazala looked outraged. "You forget your place, Mariam. Our family affairs are of no concern to you. It was a gesture of goodwill on our part to have you dine with us. Otherwise you'd be sitting with the servants."

Mrs. Haddad bristled. "It was the Shaykh's wish that I join the family for dinner. It wasn't any magnanimous gesture on your part. Don't expect me to grovel in gratitude at your feet."

Ghazala's lips tightened in anger. "Mariam, you're a paid employee here," she said in a cutting voice. "I would advise you to hold your tongue, so you don't cause further offense."

"Don't treat me like a menial servant," Mrs. Haddad's tone was just as sharp. "Gone are the days when those living in castles lorded it over the common people. I'm a modern, educated woman, not some simple serf. Yes, I earn a paycheck for the use of my brains. But I think it's a damn sight better than living like a parasite off the goodwill of a rich cousin."

There was a shocked silence.

Miftah spluttered, "How vare you? You have no vight to vay such a ving. We all vork." His words sounded so distorted with the food in his mouth that Layla felt a giggle bubbling up from her throat.

"Shut your mouth, Miftah," Ghazala snapped at her cousin. "You sound like a gibbering ape." Glaring across at the tutor, she said, "Is this how you repay our hospitality?"

"You insulted me," said Mrs. Haddad. "You have no respect for my dignity. All your self-righteous act is just for show. You all make a fuss and pretend as if you care for your cousin. But your crocodile tears don't fool me in the least. You're hoping the old man will croak soon so you can get your hands on his money."

Miftah made a choked sound and grabbed for a glass of water. A heavy frown marred his wife's sculpted features and she looked at Mrs. Haddad, her lips tight. Everyone else looked uncomfortable, except for Hala. She had a wide smile on her face.

"Your insults and insinuations will not be tolerated," Ghazala spat out at Mrs. Haddad. "How dare you make such wicked accusations?"

"I dare because I only have five weeks left before I'm gone from this cheerless castle," said Mrs. Haddad. "I'm sure you're dying to run to the Shaykh and complain about me. Well, I'm ready to pack my bags and leave tomorrow if he wants me gone. I can't wait to see the back of this place."

When Ghazala spoke again, her voice was like ice. "In consideration of the *children* at the table, I will not respond to your shameful behavior. This conversation is over."

LATER THAT EVENING, the teenagers received an unexpected summons from Shaykh Sulaiman. It was Dhul Fikar, the butler, who came up to their suites to tell them the Shaykh would like to see them. Mystified, they went downstairs and hastened to the Shaykh's suite. He was seated on a recliner in his sitting room, his feet propped on a stool. He wore a green-striped pajama suit and his color looked a little better. Qais, still clad in his white nursing uniform, sat next to him in an armchair. They were watching the news on the television.

At their entrance, Qais flicked the remote and the television screen went blank.

Adam said, "You sent for us, Shaykh Sulaiman?"

The Shaykh smiled at them. "Yes, I did." His voice sounded a bit stronger. "How would you like to go to Ghassan City tomorrow?"

Chapter Eight
At the Grand Ghassan

"**G**HASSAN CITY?" ADAM echoed. A slow smile of delight spread across his face. "That would be awesome."

"Cool," Layla crowed, her eyes alight with delight.

"That's nice." Zahra's face was wreathed in a smile.

"How come we're going?" Zaid looked curious.

"Miftah and his family are going tomorrow and coming back on Monday. I had learned from Tariq that Adam and Layla were desirous of going there. I thought it would be a good idea if you all travel together. I've spoken to Miftah and Suha. They're agreeable."

Layla's elation faded a little. She was not looking forward to being in Hala's company for the long drive.

"What time are we leaving tomorrow?" she asked.

"You'll be leaving after lunch, *insha Allah*. I've arranged for the Al-Khalili Corporation's private jet to fly you there. Instead of four hours by car, you'll get there in an hour."

A private jet? Wow!

"Once you arrive at the hotel," the Shaykh went on, "you'll be on your own and free to do whatever you wish."

"Don't worry," said Zaid. "Zahra and I will make sure Adam and Layla see some of the places we've been to."

"Excellent," said the Shaykh. "The hotel has a car service which will be at your disposal. Just call the front desk and they will arrange your ride. Is there anything else you wish to know?"

"No, I don't think so," said Layla. "Thank you so much. We're absolutely thrilled."

"I'm happy to do this for you," said the Shaykh. "You were of immense help to me last year when you found the Moon of Masarrah. This is just a small token of my gratitude."

TARIQ DID NOT seem surprised the next morning when the teenagers told him their news.

"Grandfather told me last night," he said. "You'll be zipping in and zipping out in no time with the jet. No long, tiring car ride."

"It would be nice if you could come with us too," said Adam.

"Yes, but I'm still trying to get set for my move to England. I have a lot of stuff to do, so I'll have to take a pass."

"Is the airport far from here?" said Layla.

Tariq's eyes twinkled. "There's no airport. We have an airstrip behind the limestone hills."

AT LUNCH, GHAZALA said, "Mrs. Haddad apologized to me this morning. She promised not to cause offense again. In the spirit of forgiveness, I've decided not to tell Sulaiman of her behavior. She'll be gone soon, anyway."

And good riddance too, her expression said.

"Did I miss something?" said Faisal.

"Yes, you did," Hala crowed, her mouth split into a wide grin. "Aunt Ghazzy and Mrs. Haddad had a catfight at dinner. It was like being at a boxing match." Swinging her fists in the air, she said, "Pow, pow."

"Catfight? What a vulgar expression," Ghazala said with distaste.

Faisal grinned. "I'm sorry I missed it. I should have been here."

"You keep disappearing without a word to anyone," said Miftah. "Why don't you have the decency to tell us where you're going?"

Faisal's grin turned into a scowl. "It's my business where I go. I don't have to answer to anyone."

"I'm sure Sulaiman will have something to say about that," said Miftah, his large nose in the air.

Faisal glared at his cousin. "I suppose you plan to go blabbing to him. You're nothing but a sneaky, backstabbing blabbermouth."

"*Khalas,*" said Ghazala. "That's enough. Settle your differences in private. And Faisal, please refrain from name calling in front of the children."

Tariq came to the domed hall to see the teenagers off.

"Enjoy your trip," he said. "We'll continue the riding lessons when you return, *insha Allah.*"

They followed Miftah and his family to the forecourt and boarded a brown van. The castle's chauffeur loaded their luggage while the passengers seated themselves in the ten-seater vehicle. They drove out of the gate and into the roadway, passing several limestone hills along the way. The van came to a stop at the edge of an asphalt runway. Sitting there like a graceful swan was a sleek white jet with red stripes.

As they got out of the van, they heard the powerful growling of the jet's engine. A man wearing a white uniform with white safety helmet climbed out of the cockpit and came towards them. He greeted Miftah in a familiar manner.

"This is our pilot, Fudail," Miftah yelled above the sound of the engine.

Fudail nodded to them. He was a wiry man of medium height, with a thin, sunburned face and deep lines at the corners of his eyes. He helped the chauffeur load their luggage into the jet's hold while the passengers climbed inside. There were eight luxurious leather seats, four on each side of the plush aisle. At the back was a small lavatory. After the pilot filed their flight plan with air traffic control, the jet taxied down the runway. Moments later, it rose into the air with an effortless lift of the wings.

"This is great." Adam stared out of the window. "We've never flown in such a small aircraft before."

Miftah shrugged a shoulder. "It's not much different from a regular plane."

The older man did not seem happy. His bushy brows sat close together and there was a thinness to his lips. Suha had buried her head in a magazine and as for Hala, there was a scowl on her face.

They're probably not too thrilled to have us tagging along with them.

The jet climbed steadily upward. Everything below became little blobs before disappearing altogether as the plane entered the canopy of clouds. During the flight, Miftah and Suha made a few polite remarks to the teenagers but Hala remained stand-offish. The expression on her face said they were interlopers who were not welcome. When she spoke, it was only to her father.

And all she talked about was her upcoming meeting with Uncle Saad and the places they would go shopping together.

An hour later, they touched down at a private airstrip in Ghassan City. Mustapha was there to pick them up in a black ten-seater van. He was dressed in jeans and another tightfitting T-shirt that showed his impressive muscles. With a smile on his Sumo wrestler's face, he professed himself delighted to see them all so soon.

Minutes later, they were traveling down the highway to the hotel. The skyline of Ghassan City shimmered in the early afternoon haze, a blurry sprawl of towering skyscrapers and majestic minarets. They zoomed through avenues that were wide and tree-lined and crawled through bystreets that were narrow and congested.

Mustapha drew up into the courtyard of a stately hotel that had a single dome with a golden finial atop.

"Here we are," he said. "The Grand Ghassan Hotel."

The hotel lay alongside the Ghassan Creek and was landscaped with lush green lawns and eye-catching beds of flowers. Layla knew it was just one of the many hotels owned by the Al-Khalili chain. Two bellhops took charge of their luggage and they entered the lobby, an impressive space with several sitting areas and gleaming chandeliers overhead.

Once they obtained the keys to their suites, Miftah said, "You'll be on your own now. If you need to contact me, just leave a message at the front desk. Enjoy yourselves. We'll see you around."

As the teenagers headed to the elevator, Hala said loud enough for them to hear, "I'm glad they won't be hanging around our necks anymore. I wish Uncle Sulaiman hadn't insisted they come with us."

Layla clenched her teeth. *Little witch. I'm glad we won't be seeing her mean face for the next twenty-four hours.*

Layla found their suite charming, with its scarlet and gold

décor. It had two bedrooms, a bathroom, and a small sitting room-cum-kitchenette. Sliding glass doors fringed by heavy blinds led to a shaded balcony, with a breathtaking view of the creek and its waterfront attractions. Zaid and Zahra's suite were right next door. After settling in, Adam and Layla went over to their friends' suite to make plans for that afternoon. An hour later, they were ready for their first foray into the city.

They spent the afternoon at the newest mall and returned to the hotel to have dinner at the rooftop restaurant. The sultry day had given way to a balmy evening. The rooftop restaurant was crowded, with uniform-clad waiters moving back and forth among the tables. Layla was pleased they were given a table with an unfettered view of the creek. She gazed out at the water, which reflected the dense spread of lights from around the city.

They all ordered *samak baladi* – country style fish served with thick pieces of bread. The bread was warm and crisp and the fish, fresh and succulent. As they lingered over a dessert of rice pudding topped with pistachios, conversation came around to their plans for tomorrow.

"You have to visit the Ghassan City *Souk* and the Lighthouse Mosque," said Zahra.

"And the Ibn Muqlah Gallery of Calligraphy," said Zaid.

"Sounds good to me," said Adam.

"I can't wait," said Layla.

THE TEENAGERS BREAKFASTED in the hotel's dining room the next morning before setting off on foot for the first place on their list – the Ghassan City *Souk*. Since it was only a short distance away, they had decided to walk there and arrange for the car service to pick them up in two hours. As they headed out the revolving doors of the hotel and crossed into the busy thoroughfare, Layla looked around eagerly. The streets were already bustling with life and the creek packed with sailboats. Horns blared as motorists navigated the heavy traffic.

A ten-minute walk brought them to the *souk*. It stretched before them in a never-ending sea of stalls and alleyways. The sights, the sounds and the smells were a wondrous mix of the usual and unusual. The scent of oils and food wafted through the air and the stalls were packed with a wide assortment of sparkling jewelry, clothing, toys, souvenirs and home decor. Around them, the air buzzed with the voices of vendors hawking their wares and customers haggling over prices. They listened in amusement as two vendors got into a slanging match.

"You're a clumsy camel," said the first one. "Tramp, tramp, you walk, knocking my suitcases down." He gave a comical wiggle in imitation of a camel's walk.

"It wasn't me, you bow-legged donkey," bleated the second vendor.

"If it wasn't you, then it must have been your monkey of a brother," the first vendor shot back.

The teenagers chuckled as they walked away from the two adversaries.

It was while they had stopped at a souvenir stall that Layla noticed a man watching them. He was standing at a rug display across the aisle and there was such a shifty expression on his face that she wondered if he was a pickpocket. Dressed in a gray robe, he was lean and swarthy, with a smooth-shaven face and glittering black eyes. On his left cheekbone was a thick, brown mole. His eyes bored into Layla's for a few moments before he turned on his heels and disappeared into the crowd. Layla let out a breath of relief. If he was a pickpocket, she was glad he was gone.

Laden with shopping bags containing gifts, souvenirs and other interesting mementoes, they were happy to get into the waiting car and return to the hotel. After depositing their burdens in their suites, they returned to the car. As they were boarding it, they saw a taxi pull up in front of the hotel. Hala disembarked with a multitude of shopping bags clutched in her hands. She was followed by a tall, strapping man in his mid-thirties, also carrying shopping bags.

That must be Uncle Saad who had promised to take her shopping.

Their next stop was the Ibn Muqlah Gallery of Calligraphy. Traffic heading in that direction was heavy. The car moved in fits and starts through the streets. Their excitable Asian driver took offense at the tourists darting in front of them.

"See how ze mock at me," he said in accented English. "Ze think ze are birds to fly across. When I run zem over, see how sorry ze will be."

His words made the girls burst into low giggles.

The Ibn Muqlah Gallery boasted one of the largest collections of calligraphic art in the world. The teenagers took one of the guided tours and listened with interest as the guide began his presentation. "Calligraphers have to be trained from a young age. Besides Ibn Muqlah, two other great calligraphers were Ibn Al-Bawwab and Yaqut al-Musta'simi." As they moved from display to display, he explained the different scripts used in traditional calligraphy and their origins.

As the crowd dispersed after the tour, Layla's eyes fell on a man viewing a display across the aisle. It was the swarthy man with the mole she had seen in the *souk,* the one she had thought might be a pickpocket. *Maybe I was wrong about him. He must be a tourist just like us. But still, it's a strange coincidence to see him here.*

Their next stop was the famed *Sharih Lubabah* - the Street of Innermost Essence, known for its many restaurants and bakeries. After lunching at a restaurant where the food was delicious and the service impeccable, they strolled down the sidewalk, drooling at the sweet concoctions displayed in the bakery windows. Layla's attention was caught by a man walking across the street. It was that same swarthy man with the mole again, and he seemed to be keeping pace with them. *Could it be a coincidence I'm seeing him three times now? I think not.*

"Guys, look at that man in the gray robe across the street," she said. "I saw him in the *souk* and gallery. I think he's following us."

They looked across at the Mole Man. He turned towards them at the same moment and they had a clear view of his face.

"Are you sure it's the same man?" asked Adam.

"Absolutely. Can you forget a face like that?"

"I suppose not, but it could just be a coincidence."

"I don't think so."

"Maybe he's a pickpocket waiting for a chance to snatch our purses," said Zahra, clutching her pocketbook closer.

"I thought so too. But why follow us here when he could have done it in the *souk?*"

"Some pickpockets are patient," said Zaid, "but I don't think they would follow people from place to place. Let's see if he shows up somewhere else. If he does, we'll know he's definitely following us."

They took a taxi to the Lighthouse Mosque next. The mosque was built on a scenic spot next to the sea. At the top of one of the minarets hung a great lamp that provided a guiding light to ships in the night. The teenagers strolled along the sunny promenade, admiring the view. The sea was a choppy green expanse under unblemished blue skies. Gulls and pelicans circled overhead, alighting now and then on half-submerged rocks that rose like sharp teeth.

It was Adam who spotted the Mole Man next.

They were having dessert at a Cakes & Shakes that evening and he had gone to wash off the fruit shake he had spilled on his shirt. He returned in a state of agitation.

"I just saw the Mole Man," he said. "He was sitting in a

corner, drinking a shake. I was going over to speak to him, but he bolted when he saw me. He's definitely following us."

"I knew it," said Layla in triumph. "He's up to something."

"I'd like to know what," said Zaid. "It's the weirdest thing."

Zahra wrinkled her nose. "He doesn't seem like a nice man."

"I think we've seen the last of him now," said Adam. "We're not going anywhere else after this. It's back to the oasis tomorrow."

The sun had long disappeared behind the skyscrapers as the teenagers headed to the spot where their car was waiting. At a busy intersection, they stood with a crowd of people waiting to cross the street. Several hawkers came up, peddling their wares in loud voices. Amid the noise, Zahra cried out as she stumbled and fell into the street. Everyone watched in horror as a car sped towards her, swerving to the side at the last moment and missing her by a scant two feet.

It all happened in a mere matter of seconds. Layla was still reeling from the shock as she stooped down with the boys besides their fallen companion.

"Zahra," cried Zaid. "Are you alright?"

"Yes, I think so." Zahra's voice shook as she sat up and straightened her beige scarf. "Thank Allah that car missed me."

"What happened?" asked Layla. "Did you trip or something?"

"No," said Zahra as Zaid helped her to her feet. "Someone pushed me."

Chapter Nine

Sandstorm

"WHAT?" ZAID EXCLAIMED. "Did you see who it was?"

"No, I just felt a hand shoving me in the back. The next thing I knew, I was falling down."

Layla looked around the sidewalk, but the crowd had moved on. There was no one there now.

"Are you sure someone shoved you and not jostled you by accident?" asked Adam.

"Yes." Zahra's voice was firm. "That hand pushed me very hard."

"Oh my God, you could have been killed," said Layla.

In a daze, they walked to where the car was waiting. When they reached the hotel, Zahra was still numb with shock. She did not snap out of it until she had downed two mugs of mint tea. They spent a long time discussing the harrowing incident. Who had pushed Zahra? Could it have been the sinister Mole Man who had been following them? If it was, what had been his motive? Should they report it to the police or not? In the end, they had decided against it. It would be hard to prove Zahra had been pushed. Besides, they would be leaving for Dukhan Oasis the next day and would never set eyes on the Mole Man again.

THE NEXT MORNING, Ghassan City woke up to a surprise sandstorm. In their suite, Layla heard the wind tearing around the hotel like a wild creature, slinging sand against the glass door. When Adam opened the blinds, the creek was totally obscured by a thick, beige fog. Never having been up close and personal with a sandstorm before, the brother and sister stared outside in awe. Oceans of silt and clay hung suspended, engulfing everything around in a smoky void.

The phone in their suite rang. Adam picked it up and after listening for a minute, he said, "Yes, I figured that would happen. Have you told Zaid and Zahra yet? Okay, I'll let them know. We'll see you all later."

After hanging up, he said, "That was Uncle Miftah. Our flight back to the oasis has been delayed. Instead of leaving at ten, we'll be leaving around three when the sandstorm clears. I'm calling Zaid and Zahra now to let them know."

"Tell them we'll go down for breakfast at nine," said Layla.

After speaking to their friends and hanging up the phone, Adam said, "We have two hours to go before breakfast. I'm going to get some shut-eye in the meantime."

Feeling the burn in her own eyes, Layla said, "Yeah, me too."

She returned to bed, plumped out her pillow and placed her head on it. She closed her eyes.

JUST BEFORE NINE, Zaid and Zahra knocked on Adam and Layla's door. Except for the slight pallor on her plump cheeks, Zahra seemed to have recovered from her close call with calamity. She was wearing a yellow floral dress with gray scarf, showing no outward signs of nerves. In fact, she seemed more tired than traumatized. Layla was relieved. It had been a great shock seeing that car bearing down on her friend. By a miracle of Allah, it had missed hitting Zahra.

When they went down to the dining room, Miftah and Suha were there. After filling their plates at the buffet, the teenagers politely stopped by the couple's table to give *salaams*. They were about to move on when Suha gestured to the empty chairs around their table. "You can sit here. We've got plenty of room."

She was dressed in a deep rust-colored outfit that was flattering to her buttery complexion. But it seemed as if she had not slept well. There were slight purple shadows under her eyes and a drawn look to her face. Layla found it hard to believe she was the daughter of Husam, the black sheep of the Al-Khalili family. *She hadn't even been born when the Moon of Masarrah went missing.*

After they were seated, Suha asked, "Did you have a good time yesterday?"

"We did, thank you," said Adam. "Now we know what Ghassan City looks like."

"It doesn't look like much right now with sand everywhere," said Miftah. Like his wife, he too looked like he did not have a restful night. There were small pouches beneath his eyes and his face looked blotchy. He seemed on edge, his eyes shifting restlessly around the dining room.

Hala made an entrance then. She did not look pleased to see the teenagers sitting with her father and stepmother. After filling her plate at the buffet, she had no choice but to sit with them. She was dressed in jeans and a cream lace shirt. Long earrings dangled at her ears though her face was bare of makeup. She also looked hollow-eyed with tiredness. Spreading jam on her toast, she bit into it before taking a long sip of coffee.

Trying to fill the awkward silence, Layla said, "This is the first time Adam and I are seeing a sandstorm. It's something else."

Hala's lips lifted in a sneer. "You don't have sandstorms in America? How sad. Maybe you should take some of it back in your suitcase to show your friends."

Layla's face colored at the other girl's jibe. She had to bite her tongue to hold back her retort.

Suha looked at her stepdaughter with flinty eyes. "There's no need for such rudeness, Hala. Not everywhere has sandstorms like we do."

"Stupid sandstorm," Hala muttered into her teacup. "Why did it have to happen today of all days? Uncle Saad was planning to come see us off. Now he won't be able to come."

"A *haboob* is not something anyone can control," said Suha. "Things won't always go the way we want them to. We have to learn to deal with disappointments."

"I wasn't asking for a lecture." Hala's voice was snippy. It seemed her shopping spree with Uncle Saad had not improved her temper.

"Then you shouldn't act like a spoiled child," said her stepmother.

"Just leave me alone," said Hala. "I'm tired of your constant nagging."

"That's enough, Hala." Miftah's voice sounded weary and flat.

Poor Uncle Miftah. It must be exhausting trying to keep peace between his wife and daughter.

WHEN THEY RETURNED to their suite, Adam could not sit still. He prowled about the sitting room, opening the blinds every now and then to stare out into the whirling clouds of sand. As he did so, he would drum his knuckles against the glass.

"Will you stop doing that?" Layla finally said in irritation. "It's driving me crazy."

Adam's bottom lip jutted out. "I'm going crazy cooped up in here." Dressed in black jeans and a blue Polo shirt, his hair tousled as usual, he looked like a sulky little boy.

"Why don't you and Zaid go work out in the hotel's gym?" said Layla.

Adam brightened. "That's a good idea."

As he was about to leave, he said, "I meant to ask you. What's up with you and Hala?"

"What do you mean?"

"I've seen her giving you dirty looks a few times. And this morning, she was quite nasty to you."

Layla knew if she told him about her run-in with the other girl, he might make a big fuss and even want to tell Tariq. She did not want to embarrass Tariq or escalate Hala's enmity.

"Hala doesn't seem to like me," she said truthfully. "There's nothing I can do about it."

By the time Mustapha arrived to take them to the airfield that afternoon, much of the *haboob* had receded. A light smog still lingered, smelling of soil and sand. High above, the sun's rays struggled to pierce through the layers of dust that had eclipsed it earlier. Wearing goggles and masks, they hustled out to Mustapha's van. When they reached the airfield, a dusty haze was hovering above the runway. Fudail descended from the cockpit to greet them again. The pilot seemed to take the sandstorm in stride as he went through his flight routine.

The jet roared down the runway before lifting gracefully

off the ground. It soared through sand and sky until it was cruising high above the clouds. Layla settled back against the seat for a nap. Waiting out the sandstorm had been exhausting. She wanted nothing more than to close her eyes and find a few minutes of oblivion.

The sandstorm seemed worse when they landed on the airstrip at Dukhan Oasis. Layla stared out in dismay at the blanket of sand around the limestone hills. It looked more like night than day. She had no idea how Fudail had managed to find the runway with such perfect precision.

"I thought it would be over by the time we got here," she said.

"It's usually worse inland," said Miftah. "It will probably clear by tomorrow."

The chauffeur was waiting with the brown van at the edge of the airstrip. Luggage was transferred from plane to van with quick efficiency. There were considerably more bags coming back than they had left with. Suha and Hala had done some serious shopping. They all piled into the van, the pilot included. He told them he had received instructions to stay the night at the castle. As they turned the corner at a limestone hill, Layla's eyes widened.

Dukhan Castle looked like something out of a nightmare with the sandy mist swirling around it. Two spots of light glared out from the first floor like fearsome eyes while the thick fog blanketed the top of the towers, giving the castle the look of a misshapen monster. Layla shivered. If she thought the castle had looked creepy before, it now looked positively menacing.

After entering the forecourt, they climbed out of the van, stiff and silent. The sandstorm seemed to have sucked the spirits out of them all. With dragging feet, they walked up to the front door. Dhul Fikar was there to open it and greet them. His face bore a somber look as he shuffled ahead of them into the domed hall. When they entered, it was to find Tariq,

Ghazala and Jumana sitting there, speaking in hushed tones. They became silent when the travelers walked in. Ghazala's lips had a tight look while Jumana's eyes expressed worry and some other emotion Layla could not define. As for Tariq, his jaw was clenched, as if he was holding some deep emotion in check. The travelers knew then that something had happened.

"What's wrong?" asked Miftah, his eyebrows coming together.

Lifting red-rimmed eyes in a face drawn with anguish, Tariq said, "Something terrible has happened."

Chapter Ten
Stone in a Saddle

L AYLA'S HEART SKIPPED a beat.

"What is it?" asked Suha, her eyes wide with alarm.

Tariq said, "Qais heard Grandfather's call bell going off a few minutes after twelve last night. When he got to Grandfather's suite, Grandfather's eyes were wide with shock and he was struggling to sit up. When Qais asked him what was wrong, he said he had awakened to the sound of a scream and seen the Woman in White staring down at him from the foot of the bed. She then opened the window and jumped out. After telling Qais this, Grandfather became white to the lips and passed out. Qais revived him but Grandfather's breathing was still heavy so Qais came and woke us up. We decided to take Grandfather to the hospital in Khaldun. We were in the middle of the sandstorm, but we managed to get him to the hospital without getting lost. He's there now, hooked up to tubes again." Tariq's voice ended on a choked note.

"We should never have left," said Miftah. "I shouldn't have let Hala harangue me into going to Ghassan City."

A stony look came over Hala's face at her father's words.

"Why didn't someone call us?" asked Suha.

"We didn't want you coming in the middle of the sandstorm," said Ghazala. "There was nothing you could have done. We have to wait and see what happens now. It's in Allah's hands."

That night, Layla huddled in bed as she listened to the *haboob* howl as if it would swallow up the castle. The infernal sand seemed to seep in from every crack and crevice with no respite. She could feel the gritty grains in her eyes, her nose, and even taste it on her tongue.

I don't think I want to experience another sandstorm ever again. This one is enough to last me a lifetime.

THE WIND DIED down in the night and the sandstorm was gone by the next morning. And so was the Al-Khalili Corporation's private jet. Layla heard its sharp whine over the castle just after sunrise. Fudail had wasted no time in heading back to Ghassan City.

Tariq was depressed at breakfast but at lunch, he was beaming.

"Grandfather didn't suffer another stroke or a heart attack," he said to the teenagers. "He had been suffering from shock. He's stable now and wants to come home. He threatened to stop his donations to the hospital if they didn't discharge him today. He'll be coming home this afternoon."

And so it was. The Shaykh returned to Dukhan Castle neither better nor worse than he had been before his visit from the Woman in White. As a precautionary measure, an iron bar had been placed across his window to cut off any avenue of escape should the fake ghoul feel the urge to visit his suite again.

LIFE RESUMED ITS normal course after the Shaykh's return from the hospital. And so did their riding lessons on Wednesday and Thursday. As they headed to the stables on Friday afternoon, Tariq said, "I heard there's going to be a camel race in Khaldun tomorrow. Would you like to go?"

"Oh yes," said Layla. "Adam and I have never seen a camel race before."

"It's quite an experience," said Zahra.

"And a lot of excitement," said Zaid.

"Sounds like fun," said Adam.

"It is," said Tariq. "You'll be able to see a little bit of Khaldun and get your wish to ride in my car. I have some more good news for you."

"What is is?" asked Layla.

"We're going to the fields outside. We'll ride to the Dukhan foothills."

Adam and Layla whooped in excitement.

Mounted atop their horses, the foursome followed Tariq out of the gate. They emerged onto a sandy path bordered by bitterbrush and low-lying shrubs. The surrounding landscape looked dry and gray in the harsh sunlight. It was a stark reminder they were surrounded by desert on all sides. The sky seemed even loftier in this great empty space. In the distance, the peak of the Dukhan Hills seemed to bend and shift in the concealing clouds. Nestled beneath its great hulk was a dense wall of trees.

Tariq pointed to it. "That's the acacia forest at the foothills. We're heading there. Layla and Adam, if you think we're going too fast or if you need to stop and rest, let me know."

Tariq set off at a measured trot on a well-ridden path. Layla's heart raced as she held on to Ayah's reins and guided the horse along. When they came to a gentle incline, she leaned forward in the saddle and dug her toes in the stirrups as they climbed up. The incline gave way to a flat, sandy stretch of land and Tariq broke into a canter, cuing the other horses to follow suit.

After her initial nervousness, Layla got accustomed to Ayah's rolling gait. A sense of exhilaration swept through her as the warm wind flowed over her face and the blinding rays of the sun beat down upon her back.

As they neared the acacia forest, Jasim came to a stop and reared up with a high-pitched neigh. The teenagers reined in their horses, watching in distress as Tariq clung to the great beast's back and tried to placate it. Jasim returned his forelegs to the ground but continued to fuss and stomp the ground as they looked on worriedly.

"What's the matter with him?" asked Adam.

Tariq shook his head in bewilderment. "I don't know. He's never been so fussy before."

"Maybe something startled him," said Zaid.

"I haven't seen anything that could have done so," said Tariq. He spurred the horse forward again. The next moment, Jasim's head rose up and his ears flared back. He bolted with Tariq crouched low over the saddle. The teenagers watched in shock as rider and beast disappeared into the forest.

"Oh, no," Zahra cried. "Tariq's in trouble."

"What are we going to do?" asked Layla.

"Zahra and I will go after him," said Zaid. "You and Adam can get off the horses and wait until we get back."

After Zaid and Zahra galloped away, Adam and Layla struggled to dismount without the aid of a mounting block. Layla was relieved when her feet touched solid ground again. She had been terrified the other horses would imitate Jasim and bolt too. Neither she nor Adam had the skill or experience to control a runaway horse. Layla prayed that Tariq would not be hurt. She and Adam waited in suspense, speaking soothingly to the animals as the minutes ticked by.

Fifteen minutes later, their friends appeared on the path ahead, riding at a sedate pace.

"There they are," said Layla in relief. "Thank Allah Tariq is fine."

When they were within earshot, Adam asked, "Tariq, are you okay?"

"Yes, except for my bones being a little rattled."

"How did you get Jasim to stop?" asked Layla.

"He slowed down when we got into the forest. I was able to grab hold of a tree branch and swing myself out of the saddle. Jasim came to a stop right after that."

"I wonder what made him bolt like that," said Adam.

"*This* was under his saddle." Zaid held up a sharp-edged piece of stone the size of a small hen's egg. "Since we didn't see anything on the path that would have made him bolt, I had a feeling there was something under the saddle which must be hurting him."

Adam and Layla stared at the jagged stone in surprise. They could hardly believe such a small stone would cause the great horse to bolt.

"That's weird," said Layla. "How did it get under the saddle?"

"I think someone put it there," said Zaid. "A stone doesn't suddenly appear under a saddle."

"I can't believe it was deliberate," said Tariq. "It could have gotten stuck to the saddle and whoever saddled up Jasim didn't notice it. I'll let Hatem know, but please don't mention it to anyone else. I don't want Grandfather to hear of it and worry."

As they trotted back to the stables, Layla's head swam with uneasy thoughts. *Had the stone under Tariq's saddle been an innocent oversight or had it been put there to cause him harm? If it had been placed there with deliberate intent to hurt him, who could have done it and why?*

AT DINNER, TARIQ announced their plans to attend the camel race in Khaldun the following day.

"I heard there was going to be one," said Ghazala. "I didn't realize it was tomorrow."

"You're very fortunate to see one out of season," said Miftah. "I think it's in honor of some visiting dignitary."

"Is there a special season?" asked Adam.

"It's usually from October to April," said Miftah. "The weather is much cooler during those months."

"I'm glad robots are now being used in the Emirates to replace the young jockeys," said Jumana. "I hope Ghassan will follow their example. The injuries those poor young boys face is appalling. I think I'll write a petition to get them going."

"You can't fix everything in the world, Jumana," said Suha. Her expression was calm but there had been an odd weight behind her words. She was dressed in a demure light-pink gown and wearing the same diamond pin Layla had seen her wearing before. It seemed to be one of her favorite pieces of jewelry.

"I know I can't fix everything," said Jumana. Dressed in allover black that brought out the golden glints in her amber eyes, she looked a bit exotic. "The least I can do is speak out against it so someone in a better position can make a difference."

Tariq gave her an affectionate look "That's Jum-Jum for you. Always trying to do the right thing."

"Do-gooders often get into trouble," said Faisal. He looked like a male model in stone-colored chino pants and a black button-down shirt. "Be careful of treading on the wrong toes, Jum-Jum."

Jumana threw him a cool look. "I guess I'll have to watch my step, won't I?"

"Uncle Rashid was a do-gooder too," said Tariq, a pensive look on his face. "He was always concerned about the plight of people and animals. He wasn't afraid of ruffling a few feathers to set things right."

Jumana's face lost its animation at the mention of her dead fiancé.

Faisal, who looked irritated with this turn of conversation, said, "You're making Rashid sound like a saint now, Tariq. He wasn't the paragon of virtue you make him out to be. He had his faults like everyone else. You were too blinded by hero-worship to see them."

There were several indrawn breaths of shock around the table.

Tariq's eyes kindled with anger. "I admired Uncle Rashid and I'm not ashamed to admit it. You were always jealous of him."

"Jealous?" Faisal scoffed. "If anyone was jealous, it was him."

"That's a lie," Tariq burst out. "Uncle Rashid had no reason to be jealous of you."

"That's what you think," said Faisal. "But I can tell you...."

Jumana's eyes flashed. "Stop it. Have you no respect for the dead?"

Ghazala said, "Your behavior is beyond the pale, Faisal. I'm shocked and horrified at your words."

Faisal wiped his mouth with a napkin and threw it on the table. Then he stood up and said, "And I'm sick and tired of the pack of you and your holier-than-thou attitude. You're nothing but a bunch of hypocrites." Shoving back his chair, he stormed out of the room.

Layla let out a breath after Faisal left. He was such a mercurial person - charming and pleasant one moment and mean and insulting the next. It was exhausting being around someone like him. Without his presence, the meal went on peacefully and there ensued an animated discussion of the forthcoming race and an analysis of the local dromedary contestants expected to participate. Layla and Adam, ignorant of the sport, listened attentively.

When Layla went to bed that night, it was to dream of

camels running across the desert under moonlit skies. The dream morphed into her riding Ayah, following a rider galloping towards a thick forest. The horse in front suddenly stopped and screamed in fear. Rearing up, it flung its rider to the ground before bolting into the forest. As Layla dismounted and ran to the aid of the fallen rider, she saw with horror that it was Tariq, lying as pale as death, blood seeping from a gash in his head and soaking into the ground around him.

A cloaked figure came out of the forest and said, "He was blinded by hero-worship. Now he's dead. And you're next." Moonlight flashed on metal as the cloaked figure advanced towards Layla. She screamed and began to run but no sound came from her throat, nor did she seem to be moving. Layla whimpered as the weapon flashed closer and closer. Just as the blade was about to pierce her, she woke up.

When she realized it had all been a foul dream, she felt a great sense of relief. With no saliva leaving her mouth, she spat lightly to the left and recited in Arabic, *I seek refuge in Allah from Satan, the accursed.* As the familiar words left her tongue, she offered another prayer that the nightmare was just the devil's ploy to cause distress and was not a forewarning of future events.

Chapter Eleven
Race of the Camels

THE NEXT MORNING, they boarded Tariq's Mercedes-Benz to go to the camel race in Khaldun. As they drove out of the gates, Tariq said, "I'm sorry about that scene last night. I shouldn't have let Faisal make me lose my temper."

"It's alright," said Zahra. "Faisal can be a pain sometimes."

"He apologized to me this morning," said Tariq. "And I apologized too. I don't know how long our truce will last. Knowing Faisal, it won't be for long. Well, sit back and enjoy the ride."

Layla stared out at the dusty, arid countryside. "Tariq, where does Dukhan Castle gets its water from when it's surrounded by desert?"

"We're able to tap into an underground well to water all the plants and trees. Our indoor water supply is pumped in by underground pipes from Khaldun. That water comes from the sea and we desalinate it just like they do in the Emirates."

They continued to converse until an hour later, at the top of the pass between two hills, they caught their first glimpse of Khaldun. It did not have as many skyscrapers and modern structures as Ghassan City, but it was charming, nevertheless. There were lots of congested apartment buildings surrounding places of businesses and numerous *souks*. Scattered here and there were flashy new villas among the older houses. Above walled courtyards rose the ever-present date palms.

After leaving the city precincts, they drove past groves of olives, citrus and figs, until they arrived at the great plain of the race track. In its midst stood the tent-like stadium. Adjoining it was a *souk,* a mosque, and a large building which Tariq told them housed a multitude of restrooms. After getting out of the car, Tariq opened the trunk and handed them a pair of binoculars each.

"These are for the races. There are television screens in the stadium, but you can use the binoculars for a closer look." Glancing at his watch, he said, "The race is not due to start yet. Would you like to check out the *souk* in the meantime?"

"Oh, yes," said Zahra, her eyes sparkling. She looked like a breath of fresh air in a burgundy tunic with a pink floral scarf and off-white pants.

The *souk* was smaller than the one in Ghassan City but just as packed and noisy. In one of the aisles, a gaggle of geese had escaped their cage. They ran honking and screeching, helter-skelter through the aisles, chased by their irate owner. It was a comical sight watching the man grabbing at air as the nimble geese evaded his grasping hands.

Above the din, they heard a mournful melody.

"What's that sound?" Layla looked around.

"You've got to see this for yourselves," said Tariq. "Come with me."

They crisscrossed through the narrow aisles, leaving the shade of the *souk*. They emerged into a clearing encircled by date palms and tamarisk trees. A huge crowd had gathered around the source of the music. The teenagers edged forward until they had a clear view of the proceedings. Sitting cross-legged beneath a tamarisk tree, an Indian man wearing a turban was playing the music on a bamboo flute. Next to him was an ordinary looking basket. Goosebumps broke out on Layla's skin as she sighted the large cobra slithering out from it.

Tariq said, "A few snake charmers came over from India after they were banned there."

The cobra, finally free of the basket, stood still for a few moments on the ground, its hooded head up and staring at the spectators around. Then it began to sway as if in tune to the charmer's flute. For several minutes it gyrated with sinuous grace as people threw money around it. When the last notes of the flute died away, the snake lowered itself to the ground, its hood returning to the normal shape. With deft hands, the snake charmer grasped the creature and returned it to the basket before collecting the money strewn around him.

"Yikes," Layla muttered. "That cobra totally creeped me out."

At that moment, there came a siren-like wail.

A smile spread across Tariq's face. "The races are about to start. Let's go."

Inside the stadium, Layla peered through her binoculars at the racetrack. It was protected by iron railings on both sides. At the starting line, the jockeys were getting their camels into position, and at the finishing line, a television camera stood next to an ambulance. Camel owners had taken up positions outside the railings, looks of tense anticipation on their faces. Only the dromedaries seemed unmoved by the excitement, appearing calm and contemptuous in comparison to the humans around them.

Grinning, Tariq said, "Alright, pick which camel you think will win."

After observing the camels and their jockeys for a minute, they made their choices. Layla chose a camel wearing purple, her favorite color. The race began, and the camels took off with loping strides down the racetrack. Caught up in the excitement,

Layla stood up with the others as they rooted for their favorite camels. Round and round the track the camels sped as the excitement reached fever pitch. Finally, to Zahra's delight, her camel came in first and the stadium erupted into roars.

"If we were allowed to bet, I would have made a fortune," she chortled.

After the first round of races ended, the boys went in search of snacks while the girls got up to stretch their legs.

Zahra clutched Layla's hand. "Look, it's the Mole Man. He's here."

"Where?"

"Over in the next aisle."

Layla turned and saw the sinister man hurrying down the aisle. He was dressed in a dark-brown robe.

"I can't believe he's here," she said. "I thought we'd never see him again."

"Do you think he followed us here?" Zahra's eyes looked huge in her face.

"There's only one way to find out. We're going to ask him."

"Do you think it's safe to go after him?"

"Yes, there are people everywhere. There's not much he can do."

The two girls took off after the Mole Man as he exited the stadium and headed towards the *souk*.

"He's going to the *souk*," said Zahra. "I don't think we should go after him."

"If we don't, how else are we going to talk to him?"

"We don't talk to him. We stay away from him."

"No, we have to find out why he's following us."

Zahra came to a stop, a stubborn look on her face. "I think it's a bad idea. I don't want to go."

Layla eyed her friend in irritation. "Look, why don't you go find the boys and bring them to the *souk*? In the meantime, I'll keep our man in sight."

"You're being pigheaded." Zahra glowered at her.

"And you're being unreasonable."

"Fine, go then," said Zahra, losing patience. "But for heaven's sake, be careful. I'll bring the boys over as soon as I find them." She turned and ran back in the direction of the stadium.

Layla rolled her eyes and went after the Mole Man. She kept pace with him all the way into the *souk*. The place was practically deserted as most of the vendors had closed shop and gone to see the races. Those that remained either had their heads buried in newspapers or were napping. Ignoring the little voice of reason that told her to heed Zahra's warning and go back to the stadium, Layla continued shadowing the Mole Man. He came to a large food court. It was empty of people but filled with tables and chairs. A series of restaurants were set in a semi-circle around it. Layla sniffed appreciatively at the delicious smell of food being prepared behind the scenes.

A small, nondescript man stood up to meet the Mole Man. The man was dressed in a crumpled beige robe and had darting eyes and a nervous manner. The Mole Man sat down next to him and after exchanging a few low words, the man handed the Mole Man a folded piece of paper. The latter glanced briefly at it before tucking it in a pocket of his robe.

Hoping Zahra and the boys would appear at any moment, Layla marched up to the two men. They swung around to look at her and she saw the light of recognition in the Mole Man's eyes.

"Why have you been following me and my friends?" she demanded.

The Mole Man's expression darkened in displeasure. He said a few words to his companion in a language Layla did not understand. Both men got up from the table and hurried out of the food court. The man in the beige robe slinked away to the right, while the Mole Man headed left. Layla gritted her teeth and took off after him.

"Wait," she called out, almost running to keep up with his long strides. "You didn't answer my question."

Ignoring her, the Mole Man strode into an aisle containing ice buckets. As Layla followed, he kicked one of them towards her before striding away. Dodging the bucket, Layla continued after him. *So much for me thinking he won't try a dirty trick. He's not going to get rid of me that easily. I'll follow him until he goes down a hole or something. I hope Zahra and the boys show up soon.*

The Mole Man turned back and saw Layla still on his heels. His eyes darted around, settling on a fruit and vegetable stall nearby. The owner was reclining on a cushioned chair, head thrown back and mouth open in what looked to be deep sleep. There was no one else nearby. As Layla looked warily at her quarry, he grabbed a fat tomato off the stall. Before she could deduce his intent, he threw it forcefully in her direction.

Layla tried to duck but the man's aim was unerring. The soft, overripe tomato hit her in the middle of the forehead with a dull smack, bursting apart and spilling juice in her eyes and face. Startled and blinded for a moment, Layla came to a stop and wiped the juice from her eyes with the tail of her fuchsia scarf.

Seething with fury now and with her eyes smarting from the tomato juice, she took off after the Mole Man with even more determination. If he thought tossing a tomato at her would scare her, he would soon learn otherwise. He was now heading to the clearing at the back of the *souk* where the snake charmer's cobra had danced earlier. Upon reaching the clearing, Layla saw the Indian man taking a nap under the tamarisk tree, his harmless-looking basket next to him. The Mole Man came to a stop beside the snake charmer and stared at Layla with a look of malevolence.

Refusing to be browbeaten by the brute, she squared her

shoulders and moved towards him. He watched her like a wild animal eyeing its prey. Layla never imagined for a moment he would do what he did next. Bending swiftly, he picked up the snake charmer's basket. Then with a look of gloating triumph on his face, he hurled it at her. Layla froze as the basket sailed through the air and landed in front of her. She screamed as it sprung open, ejecting the cobra inches from her feet.

Chapter Twelve
Pieces of Paper

THE MOLE MAN made good his escape as Layla stared petrified at the rearing, hissing cobra in front of her. She had seen enough of animal shows to know cobras could move with lighting swiftness at the slightest movement, sinking their venomous fangs into their hapless prey. She stood rooted to the spot, staring almost hypnotically into the obsidian eyes of the monstrous serpent as the blood in her veins alternated between hot and cold. Time ceased to matter as she was held in the grips of a mind-numbing fear such as she had never felt before. Her only thought in that stricken state was to be as still as a statue so the loathsome viper would not have cause to strike.

Had she dared to take her eyes off the cobra for a second, she would have seen the snake charmer creeping ludicrously on his hands and knees to grasp his empty basket. All she saw was the basket descending over the cobra's head, breaking the hypnotic hold of the creature and freeing her from its ghastly spell. Layla sagged in relief and would have collapsed to the ground had Adam not materialized beside her and wrapped his arms around her nerveless body.

"I've got you," he said. "Are you okay?"

She managed to say, "Yes. I guess today's not my day to be cobra food."

"That was horrible," said Zahra, her chubby cheeks drained of color. "We were looking everywhere for you. Then we heard you scream and came here. I almost fainted when I saw that cobra in front of you."

"You were right about the Mole Man," said Layla. "I should have listened to you."

"Tell us what happened," said Zaid. "We already told Tariq about the Mole Man following us in Ghassan City."

Layla told them what had transpired in the *souk* before they came on the scene.

Tariq listened with a dawning look of distress on his face. "I don't know why this man is following you and trying to hurt you. Let's go look for him. Maybe he'll talk when he sees all of us."

"He's probably gone by now," said Layla. "I don't think he'd stick around after his disgusting deed." Now that she was over her fright, Layla was livid. She wished they could get their hands on the villain, so they could drag the truth out of him.

"Why in the world did you chase after that lunatic?" asked Adam. "That cobra could have killed you."

A barrage of strange words came from the snake charmer, who was now sitting with his basket under a date palm a few feet away.

"What's he saying?" asked Zaid.

"I'll go ask him," said Tariq.

After several minutes of back and forth with the snake charmer, Tariq returned.

"What did he say?" asked Zahra.

"He told me in really terrible Arabic that his cobra can't harm anyone."

"Oh, please," said Adam. "A snake is a snake. What makes him think his cobra is any different?"

Tariq grinned. "Its poisonous fangs have been removed."

"You mean I wouldn't have died if it had bitten me?" asked Layla.

"No, it has no poison left," said Zaid. "I've read about snake charmers defanging their cobras. No wonder our man doesn't seem too concerned."

The snake charmer must have heard and understood what they were saying. He let loose another stream of words in his native tongue. Tariq went over to speak to him again and after much hand gestures and low mumblings from the snake charmer, he returned. "Our man said his cobra is so frightened it might not dance for the rest of the day."

"That hideous serpent is frightened?!" said Layla. "You could have fooled me. I still feel like a quivering hunk of jelly."

"Let's go back to the stadium and get you some juice," said Adam.

Tariq looked at his watch. "The last race just ended. Everyone will be leaving. Let's go see if we can find this Mole Man there. We'll have lunch afterwards."

When they came out of the *souk,* a thin trickle of spectators was exiting the stadium. By the time they reached the doors, people were pouring out in thick streams. The teenagers stood to the side, gazing at the sea of faces around them. They stiffened when they saw a familiar figure pushing his way through the slowly moving snarl of people. It was the Mole Man and he saw them the same moment they saw him.

Adam shouted, "There he is! After him."

As the teenagers threaded their way through the crowd, the Mole Man gave them a look of malice and began shoving people out of his path. When he finally forced his way out, he picked up his robes and ran towards the parking lot. By the time his pursuers untangled themselves from the crowd, the Mole Man was way ahead of them. As he reached the parking lot, a white object flapped out of his robe. It sailed backwards, landing under the wheels of a black Toyota Tundra. The man did not seem to notice. He reached a dusty blue Nissan Pathfinder and yanked open the door.

"Oh, no," Zaid panted, "He's getting away." Even though they put on an extra spurt of speed, they were too late. They came to a stop and watched as the Mole Man accelerated away with a screech of tires. They were too far away to get a reading of the license plate.

Tariq pointed to the Toyota Tundra. "Something fell out of his robe and went under that car. Maybe it will give us a clue about him." Going over to the vehicle, he stooped and picked up a thin white object.

"It's a piece of paper," he said, holding up the folded square.

"It must be the note the man in the *souk* gave to him," said Layla. "What does it say?"

Tariq opened the paper and held it aloft so they all could read it. It bore several typewritten sentences. After reading it, they looked at one another in puzzlement.

"It makes no sense," said Tariq. "The words are all jumbled."

"I think it's a cipher," said Zaid, his face lighting up with interest. "I got interested in them after our adventure at Bayan House last year. If I can figure out the pattern of the cryptogram, I can decode what's written here. I hope it won't require a special key."

"Leave it until we get back home," said Tariq. "Let's go have lunch now."

They bought lunch at the food court and found an empty table. As they ate, conversation centered around the Mole Man and what could be the reason for his strange behavior.

"We won't know what he's up to unless we question him," said Adam. "To do that, we need to find him. He seems to be a very slippery character."

"Maybe he's staying at a hotel in Khaldun," said Tariq. "We can check a few of them today to see if he's there. If not, we can return another day and check a few more until we've checked them all."

"He might be staying with friends or relatives and not at a hotel," said Zaid. "Or he could be on his way out of Khaldun right now."

"I think we should check the hotels," said Layla, taking a bite of her *falafel*. "I'd like to know what that man is up to." Glancing at her once pristine scarf, now stained with tomato juice and seeds, she said, "I have to wash my scarf as soon as we get back home before it starts growing tomatoes."

Zahra said, "Zaid, can you do a sketch of the Mole Man for us to show at the hotels? It would be easier than describing him every time."

Zaid nodded. "I'll give it a try."

From their adventure last year, Layla knew he was quite talented at sketching.

"Let's do that in the car," said Tariq. "It will save us some time."

Back in the car, Tariq gave pencil and notepaper to Zaid. By the time they entered the city center, Zaid had sketched an amazing likeness of the Mole Man. It yielded no results at the first three hotels they checked. Tired and sweaty from their quest, they decided to give up the search for the day.

While walking back to Tariq's car, they saw an old woman seated on a bench under the awning of a clothing store. Her dark hair was sprinkled with gray and fell in a single plait down her back. She wore a faded dark-blue gown with a red shawl slung over her shoulders. She was shuffling a pack of cards with great expertise. With her leathery brown skin and hooked nose, she was the epitome of a fairy tale witch.

"Would you like me to tell you your fortunes?" she croaked as they passed by.

When Tariq politely declined, the woman muttered words in a strange tongue.

"Is she putting a curse on us or something?" asked Layla.

"No, she was speaking in *Domari*. She's a gypsy," said Tariq.

Adam chuckled. "Maybe we should ask her to look in her crystal ball and find the Mole Man for us."

"If fortune tellers really knew the unseen or unknown, they'd all be rich and famous," said Zaid. "I don't understand how people get fooled by them."

"Maybe we should show her the sketch and ask her if she knows the Mole Man," said Zahra. "She looks very observant."

"That's a good idea," Tariq agreed.

They retraced their steps to the gypsy woman. She looked up at them, her eyes bright and eager. Zaid showed her the sketch and asked, "Can you please tell us if you know this man?"

The gypsy woman took the sketch from him and peered at it. A look of terror came over her face. *"Al-Aqrab,"* she gasped, dropping the sketch as if it had become red hot.

Muttering under her breath in *Domari,* she elbowed them aside and took off down the street. The teenagers stared after her until she turned a corner and disappeared.

"What in the world," Layla exclaimed. "I guess she knows our Mole Man."

"And is terrified of him," said Adam.

"She called him The Scorpion," said Zahra.

"It's probably a nickname," said Zaid. "At least one person in this city seems to know our man."

"Al-Aqrab," Layla repeated. "I've heard that name before, but I'm not sure where."

"I wonder why she's so afraid of him," said Adam.

"That we shall soon find out," Tariq promised. "We'll come back another day and our bird will sing for us."

Layla laughed, her dimples flashing. "You've seen too many bad gangster movies."

WHEN THEY GOT back to the castle, they decided to rest a bit before gathering in Zaid's suite to figure out the coded message. When she got to her room, Layla scrubbed the tomato remnants from her scarf and hung it out to dry. Changing into a soft cotton nightdress, she gave a great sigh of relief as her head hit the pillow and her body sank into the soft mattress.

Later, when she went over to Zaid's room, the others were already there. Tariq came in right behind her, Bilqis at his heels. The cat's gaze flicked around the room, her tail making patterns behind her. She found a dark corner, curled herself up and went to sleep.

Adam grinned. "Now that Her Royal Highness, the Queen of Sheba, is fast asleep, I guess we can get down to business. Bring out that piece of paper, Zaid."

Zaid held up the piece of paper. "I've already decoded it."

"That was quick work," said Tariq in admiration.

"It wasn't really difficult," said Zaid, modest as always. "It's written in a simple code known as a Caesar Cipher. Each letter represents another letter at certain fixed points of the alphabet. When you put the letters together, they form the plain text of the message."

"What does it say?" said Zahra.

"It says, *Bird to be caught next Thursday night at nine. Select the catchers and prepare the cage.*"

"Hmm, that sounds suspicious," said Layla. "Our Mole Man, a.k.a. *Al-Aqrab*, is definitely up to no good."

"I didn't think people used coded messages anymore now that there are cell phones," said Adam.

"Cell phones leave electronic traces," said Zaid. "I guess whoever wrote this message didn't want that."

Layla sighed. "We're no closer to knowing why *Al-Aqrab* has been following us. I wish I could remember where I heard that name before."

"Do you think it was here or in Ghassan City?" asked Zahra.

"I have no idea. All I know is, I heard it somewhere before."

"We need to speak with that gypsy woman again," said Adam. "She knows who he is and can tell us about him."

"Do you think we can go back tomorrow, Tariq?" asked Layla.

Tariq, who was wearing a faraway look on his face, seemed not to hear her.

Layla waved a hand in front of him. "Earth to Tariq."

Tariq blinked. "I'm sorry, what were you saying?"

Layla repeated her question and Tariq said, "Yes, we can go tomorrow afternoon, *insha Allah*. We can leave at two to get an early start, if you wouldn't mind giving up your rest."

"Not at all," said Zaid.

"Is something wrong, Tariq?" asked Zahra. "You had a weird look on your face just now."

Tariq said slowly, "Thinking of this piece of paper gave me a flashback of what Uncle Rashid said the night he visited me. I'm sure he mentioned something about paper. I've tried to remember exactly what but I'm drawing a blank."

"Yeah, I know that feeling," said Layla. "Keep trying."

Tariq stood up. "I will. I must go now. I promised Grandfather I would tell him about the races. Bilqis, let's go, *habibi*."

Bilqis opened her eyes, stood up and stretched. She walked regally out the door with her owner.

Layla leaned back against the couch and closed her eyes. "*Al-Aqrab, Al-Aqrab,*" she muttered. "Where in the world did I hear that name before?"

"It doesn't matter where you heard it," said Adam. "All that matters now is finding that lunatic and learning what he's up to."

Chapter Thirteen
The Sign of the Scorpion

O N THE WAY to Khaldun the next afternoon, Layla said, "How are we going to get the gypsy woman to talk to us? She might bolt again."

"Leave it to me," said Tariq. "I know what might loosen her tongue."

It was a little after three when they reached Khaldun. They found the gypsy woman sitting in the same spot she was the previous day. At first, she did not notice them. She was busy reading the fortune of a couple who tossed her a few bills before proceeding on their way. When she became aware of their presence, her eyes widened. She stared at them like a mouse would at a prowling cat.

Tariq smiled brightly at her. "Good afternoon. We've come to ask for your help."

The gypsy woman shook her head and muttered, "I know nothing. I can't help you."

"You know who *Al-Aqrab* is," said Zaid. "Won't you tell us about him?"

The gypsy woman flinched, her eyes darting around fearfully. "I know nothing," she repeated. "You're wasting your time here."

Layla gnashed her teeth in frustration. It was clear the gypsy woman was lying.

Tariq held up a roll of bills in front of the fearful woman. "All this will be yours if you tell us about *Al-Aqrab.*"

The gypsy woman licked her lips as if she had sighted a rare delicacy she had not tasted in ages. The teenagers hoped the money would soften her stance. They could see her desire for it warring with her fear of *Al-Aqrab.* It was a tense moment as they waited for her to make her choice. She finally did, and they relaxed at her next words.

"I can't talk to you here," she mumbled. "Go to my house at Number Eleven Hamdani Street. It's five blocks away between Rida and Burda Streets. Wait in the courtyard. I'll leave in a few minutes and meet you there."

As they headed back to the car, Zahra said, "I feel bad she has to walk in the sun and we'll be riding in the car."

"She wouldn't have come if we had offered her a ride," said Adam. "She's afraid *Al-Aqrab* is watching."

Tariq drove slowly. It was soon apparent they were in one of the most squalid parts of Khaldun. The streets were cracked and potholed while walls enclosing courtyards were crumbling or in need of painting.

Zaid, who had been keeping track of their progress, said, "We're in Hamdani Street now."

"Let me park and we'll look for the house," said Tariq. "I see an empty spot to our right."

They got out of the car, watching warily as a lean, mangy dog sniffed at a pile of garbage a few feet away. Finding nothing to eat, it gave a whimper and moved on to sniff at another pile. In one of the courtyards, a cat sat in the sun washing itself. It was a wizened, skeletal creature that looked as if it had not eaten a meal in ages. Layla's heart was filled with pity to see such malnourished animals.

"I wish," she said, "that all people and animals in the world had enough food to eat and never have to go hungry." Pointing to the dog and cat, she said, "Look at how starved those animals look. Are the people around here that poor, Tariq?"

Tariq sighed. "Yes, they are. Gypsies live in this neighborhood and people give them a hard time when it comes to jobs. Grandfather has hired some of them to work in the stables and orchard but not everyone is willing to let go of their fears and do the same. He also donates regularly to the organizations in Khaldun that help the gypsies. He's very generous with his money. Once, I heard Uncle Miftah say there might be nothing left for them if Grandfather gives away so much. When I told Grandfather about it, he said, 'They haven't learned yet, the more you give the more you get.'"

"Your grandfather is a wise man," said Zaid.

Number Eleven was a shabby white villa which had become discolored with age. Through a creaking iron gate, they entered a courtyard that had more cracks than they could count. They stood under the shade of the single, straggly date palm. It leaned oddly to the side, as if bent with old age. As the minutes ticked by, Layla wondered if the gypsy woman had played a cunning trick on them. The next moment, the gate creaked open and she came hurrying into the courtyard, her red shawl slung over her head and shoulders.

Opening the front door, she took a quick, nervous look into the street before beckoning them in. They found themselves in a small sitting room with faded yellow curtains and a threadbare rug. Two worn sofas, a small coffee table, and a rocking chair were the only furniture. Against the wall was a small television set on a stand. The gypsy woman pointed them towards the sofas before seating herself in the rocking chair.

"My name is Aini," she said, looking at them with eyes that

told a tale of suffering and struggle. "What do you want to know about *Al-Aqrab?*" She flinched as she said the name.

"Who is he?" asked Tariq.

Aini's face became grim. "He's the kingpin of a network that preys upon people. They steal valuable jewelry, paintings and antiquities, and they kidnap wealthy people for huge ransoms. They also kill anyone who gets in their way."

The teenagers exchanged alarmed looks at this piece of information.

"How do you know this?" said Layla.

The gypsy woman gave a twisted smile. "I've made it my business to learn about him after he murdered my husband."

"He murdered your husband?" Zahra looked aghast.

"Yes. It all started two and a half years ago when my husband, Naji, found a job as a taxi driver with the help of a friend. It was a well-paying job and Naji was happy to be working after long months of unemployment. In return for finding him the job, the friend would ask him from time to time to deliver sealed messages or pick up and drop off passengers. One day, the friend asked him to take a passenger to a villa outside the city. Naji picked up the man, who carried several shopping bags with him. When they arrived at the villa, the passenger got out with his bags and told Naji to wait for him, that he would be back in fifteen minutes. Naji said the man seemed ill at ease but he didn't think anything of it at the time. After the man left, Naji felt thirsty, so he went to the trunk to get a bottle of water. That's when he noticed a small shopping bag lying at the foot of the back seat. He thought the man must have left it behind by mistake. He decided he would take it to the villa. He opened the door and picked up the bag. When he heard glass striking against glass, he was curious to know what was inside, so he opened the bag. What he saw shocked him so much he dropped the bag down in fright and shut the door. Feeling flustered, he went back to his seat."

"What did he see?" asked Zahra.

"He saw two glass jars with holes on the lids. Each one held a black scorpion."

Layla grimaced. "Ugh"

"What happened next?" asked Adam.

"The passenger came running back to the car and said he had forgotten a bag. Naji said nothing. He didn't want the man to think he had been poking his nose where it didn't belong. He wondered what the man planned to do with the scorpions but didn't want to ask. The man returned twenty minutes later, looking even more nervous. Naji brought him back to the city. That night, we saw on the news that a mother and her three-year-old daughter had been stung to death by scorpions. They showed a shot of the house where it had happened. Naji got his second shock of the day. It was the villa where he had taken the passenger. He was disturbed as you can imagine, so he called his friend."

"What did the friend say?" asked Tariq.

"The so-called friend told Naji to keep his mouth shut or he would feel *Al-Aqrab's* sting just like the mother and daughter had done. When Naji asked who *Al-Aqrab* was, he told Naji that *Al-Aqrab* was their employer and he didn't like traitors. Naji said he didn't care who *Al-Aqrab* was, that he would go to the police the next day and report what he had seen. The next morning, I left to go to the *souk*. When I came back, I found Naji in the courtyard with a knife in his heart and a dead scorpion in his hand. It was the sign of *Al-Aqrab*. When I confronted the so-called friend, he told me *Al-Aqrab* had given the order for Naji's murder. And if I go to the police or speak to anyone about *Al-Aqrab*, I will be next. Fearing for my life, I kept quiet. Then you showed me the drawing of the one with the mole on his cheek. The so-called friend. I haven't seen or heard from him since Naji's murder. But now he has come back to punish me. He's *Al-Aqrab's* loyal henchman."

"*Al-Aqrab's* henchman?" Zaid repeated. "You mean the one with the mole is not *Al-Aqrab?*"

"Of course not," said Aini. "No one knows who *Al-Aqrab* is. He's the puppet master pulling the strings behind the scenes. Why are you interested in the one with the mole?"

"He's been following us, and we wanted to know why," said Layla.

The gypsy woman looked alarmed. "The one with the mole has been following you?"

Adam told her about the Mole Man following them in Ghassan City and his despicable deed of throwing the cobra at Layla. "After he escaped, we decided to show his sketch at a few hotels to see if anyone knew him. We didn't have any luck, that's how we ended up asking you."

"Why do you think the one with the mole has come back to punish you?" asked Zahra.

The gypsy woman slumped in the rocking chair, her leathery brown face haggard. "I've been asking questions about *Al-Aqrab*. There are some among my people who know about him. At first, I kept my mouth shut but my eyes and ears open. I wanted to learn as much as I could about my husband's murderer, so I could bring about his downfall one day. That's how I learned those things about him. Two weeks ago, our tribe gathered one night to celebrate the birth of a child. I overheard my tribesmen talking around the fire about *Al-Aqrab*. They were saying he was from a rich and powerful family. That he has a tattoo of a scorpion on his upper arm and hundreds of scorpions at his disposal. After hearing this, I asked them if they knew who he was and where he could be found. They told me I shouldn't ask such questions. I told them they were shielding a murderer, that *Al-Aqrab* was using our people for his own evil ends. They became angry and said *Al-Aqrab* is the friend of the gypsies and helps them when everyone else shuns them, that *Al-Aqrab* would cut out my tongue if I didn't stop talking about him.

When you showed me the picture of the one with the mole, I thought *Al-Aqrab* had sent him to punish me. That's why I got scared and ran away."

"Oh Aini, we're sorry you had such a fright," said Layla.

"I hope *Al-Aqrab* doesn't find out you've been here to see me." The gypsy woman looked terrified again. "There's no knowing what he might do to both you and me."

Layla felt a cold chill race up her spine at Aini's words. *The gypsy woman must be exaggerating. We're a bunch of teenagers who know nothing about Al-Aqrab. Why would he want to harm us?*

Tariq said, "Thank you for telling us your story, Aini. We appreciate it." He handed her the wad of notes and she took it with a quick smile, the lines of worry easing on her face.

After leaving Aini's sad little house, Adam said, "I wonder if she's telling the truth or came up with that story to make some money."

"She's scared of *Al-Aqrab,*" said Zaid. "She's not faking that."

"We still don't know why the Mole Man has been following us," said Zahra.

"Yes, that's still a mystery," said Layla.

"I don't like it," said Tariq. "There's something going on here that worries me."

THAT NIGHT, THE teenagers were in Layla's suite watching an episode of Desert Dilemmas when there came a knock at the door. Tariq entered, the collar of his shirt askew and his curly hair sticking out as if he had been running his fingers through it. His eyes were wide, and the color seemed to be drained from his face.

"What's the matter?" asked Layla. "It's not your grandfather, is it?"

"No, no, Grandfather's fine."

"What it it then?" asked Zaid.

"I found a scorpion on my bed."

Chapter Fourteen
A Scream in a Dream

"**A** SCORPION?!" THEY EXCLAIMED in unison.

"Yes. A black, poisonous one. Bilqis saw it and started hissing. It might have bitten me if she hadn't seen it."

"Oh, that's an awful thought," said Zahra.

"What did you do with it?" asked Adam.

"I killed it with a hairbrush. I don't know how it got into my room. They don't usually come into living areas. They're not even common around these parts."

They stared at one another as the truth dawned upon them.

Adam said, "It's the sign of *Al-Aqrab*. He must have had someone put the scorpion on your bed."

Layla exclaimed, "I just remembered where I heard that name before."

"Where?" asked Zahra.

"In the grove, when the man and woman were arguing that night."

"Are you sure?" asked Tariq.

Layla nodded. "Yes, I'm sure."

"What does it all mean?" asked Zahra.

"It could be that *Al-Aqrab* is after you, Tariq." Zaid's face was grave. "And those people Layla heard in the grove must be his accomplices. They must have planted the stone in Jasim's saddle and the scorpion on your bed. It can't be just a coincidence. Maybe he's the one who murdered Rashid too. And has the Woman in White scaring everyone."

"If that's true, why was the Mole Man following you?" asked Tariq.

"I don't know," said Zaid. "I think we're mixed up somehow."

"What are we going to do?" asked Zahra.

"We'll have to be on our guard from now on," said Adam. "And check our beds every night to make sure no scorpions are lying in wait."

THE MOON WAS a pale blur in a purple-hued sky as Layla slipped through the inner courtyard and headed towards the back of the castle. A gusty wind, laden with the scent of jasmine and roses, whipped at the branches of the olive and date palms, sending them sashaying back and forth. When she came to the fork at the rear of the courtyard, she veered left and walked until she beheld the lone tower looming in front of her, dark and dismal in the night. A flare of light at the top drew her gaze and she hastened towards it, filled with a sense of urgency. Suddenly, her feet became rooted to the spot and she found herself unable to move. She cried out in panic, flailing her arms as she fought against the unseen force holding her back. The next moment, an agonized scream tore through the silence, piercing her to the soul and stilling her struggle against the vise that trapped her. As she watched in horror, a dark shape hurtled out of the window and hit the ground with a sickening crunch. The next moment, a scurrying sound came to her ears and she stared petrified as a sea of black scorpions crawled towards the body.

Layla awoke in the aftermath of the awful dream, her heart racing in fright and goosebumps pebbling her skin. Pushing aside the covers, she sat up and switched on the bedside lamp. She breathed easier as the warm glow lit up the room, chasing away the lingering remnants of her nightmare. After whispering a prayer, she glanced at her bedside clock. It was just after twelve. The night was still young. She only hoped she would be able to go back to sleep after that terrifying dream. As she settled back against the pillows, there came a knock at her door and Adam's voice floated into her bedchamber.

"Layla, are you awake?"

"Yes, I am."

"I guess you heard the scream too. We're going down to the grove to look for the Woman in White. Hurry up and come."

"I'll be right there."

That scream in my dream had been real. I wonder why the Woman in White is paying us such special attention? Is it at Al-Aqrab's request?

Layla scrambled off the bed and started to get dressed. Bundling her coil of hair in a scrunchy, she dragged on the blue scarf she had worn earlier and pulled on a black *abaya* over her nightdress. She joined the others in the corridor and followed them down the stairway. Adam had brought a comb. He wedged it in the door to keep it from locking. No animal would be able to squeeze into the small space. They entered the grove.

A thin sliver of moon lit the night sky, sneaking in strips of light through the branches of the leafy *ghafs*. The bulky trees stirred gently.

If only trees could talk, they would have told us who the Woman in White was.

"I feel like a spy," Zahra whispered as they made their way through the undergrowth. After traversing the grove, they saw no signs of the Woman in White.

"She's gone," said Zaid. "She must have left right after she screamed. It's no use looking anymore. I doubt she'll come back."

"She screamed really loud," said Zahra. "It sounded like she was just outside the window."

Zahra's words jogged Layla's memory.

"I thought about that the second time I heard her scream," said Layla. "Then I forgot about it. Unless our windows are open, we shouldn't hear her so clearly."

"She could be using an amplifier," said Zaid. "A bullhorn would give her the volume to make her screams sound so creepy."

"That must be her little trick," said Adam. "Quite smart of her, I must say."

"If she's working for *Al-Aqrab*, she must have a few tricks up her sleeve," said Layla.

As they were about to return to the stairs, they froze when they heard the slow tread of footsteps coming into the grove.

"Quick, behind the bushes," Adam whispered. They crouched behind the low-lying shrubbery and listened as the footsteps drew nearer. Peering from their hiding place, they watched as a figure in a dark cloak headed to the back of the grove, sidestepping tree trunks and undergrowth along the way.

"That's the cloaked figure I saw that night," said Layla.

"Let's follow him," said Zaid.

"Okay, but quietly," said Adam. "We don't want him to hear us."

The teenagers slinked after the Cloaked Man until he came to the castle's wall. He opened a gate and went through it, closing it behind him.

Adam signaled to them to step away from the gate.

After they were a safe distance away, he said, "We can't take the risk of following him. He might be just outside."

"I wonder who he is," said Zaid. "And what he's doing creeping about here."

"Maybe he's *Al-Aqrab* accomplice too," said Layla. "They could all be working together."

THEY FOUND TARIQ alone at breakfast the next morning and told him about chasing after the Woman in White last night and coming across the Cloaked Man. Tariq looked troubled when they were done.

"I know you find it exciting," he said, "but please be careful. If they're *Al-Aqrab's* accomplices, they're dangerous and you could get hurt."

"We won't take any chances," Adam promised.

Before Tariq left the sunroom, he said, "Can you meet me at the stables a little earlier this afternoon? About two should be fine. We'll take the horses to the foothills again. After we return and have refreshments, there's a special place I want to show you."

"Ooh, which place is that?" asked Layla.

Tariq chuckled. "It's a surprise. I'll see you at two."

After breakfast, the teenagers visited Shaykh Sulaiman, who was happy to see them. They spent some time in the recreation area before Adam suggested splitting up and looking for any suspicious activity.

"I'll take a look at the postern gate in the grove and see what's outside," he said. "Then I'll hang around the inner courtyard."

Zahra said, "I'll take the forecourt."

"I'll go down to the stables," said Zaid.

"And I'll take a look at the third floor inside the castle," said Layla. "I want to find the spot where the Woman in White was standing the night we came."

"Let's meet in my suite before lunch to compare notes," said Adam.

After the teenagers split up, Layla headed into the castle. She felt as if she was in another world as she climbed the dim stairway and stood on the even dimmer landing of the third floor. Shafts of sunlight came through the windows at the end of the hallways, revealing wispy cobwebs and dancing dust motes. She found the spot overlooking the forecourt where the Woman in White had stood on the night of their arrival. There was a jumble of shoe prints in the dust.

"Aha, Woman in White," she said. "This proves you're no ghoul, if ever there was any doubt. You're flesh and blood alright, and we're going to catch you soon."

Layla wandered around the empty, dusty chambers. The third level of the castle looked like the inside of an abandoned old house. *It's a pity all this space is going to waste.* She was about to descend the stairs to return downstairs when she saw a strange sight before her.

On the gallery above the stairs, green polyester curtains hung from one end of the wall to the other. It was very odd, considering no windows were there. Curious, Layla walked over and pulled aside one of the panels. The grommets slid across the rod and the curtains parted to reveal a most surprising sight. It was a portrait gallery of the Al-Khalili family.

Layla recognized the people of the household at once. Shaykh Sulaiman was there as well as Tariq, the cousins, and several other men and women whose relationship to the household she could not determine. Finally, she stared at the portrait of a man that bore a startling resemblance to Faisal. He had the same striking bone structure but had dark eyes, straight hair and a neatly clipped beard. His smiling countenance was unlike Faisal's brooding demeanor.

Rashid.

She stared at his picture, feeling immensely sad he had met such a tragic end. *Had he really been murdered as Tariq thought? Was his murderer now targeting Tariq? How do we fit into the picture? Why was Al-Aqrab's henchman following us? And why is the Woman in White trying to scare us? Is the Cloaked Man in cahoots with them?*

Lost in her morbid thoughts, she closed the curtains and descended the stairs.

"What are you doing here?" The harsh query startled Layla out of her reverie. She looked down to see Hala scowling at her at the foot of the stairs.

"I went up to explore the third floor," she said, annoyed at the other girl's tone. "Tariq said we could look around whenever we want."

"You're making yourself quite at home here, aren't you?" Hala's voice had a spiteful bite.

"What's that supposed to mean?"

"Maybe you think you'll be living here one day."

"You're crazy." Layla's voice was cold as she reached the last stair and stood eye to eye with the antagonistic girl. "Tariq is nothing more than a friend to me."

"Like I believe you," Hala sneered.

Layla felt a hot rush of anger. "I don't care. You're the one who's chasing after him, not me. Stop being so pathetic."

"How dare you." Hala's face filled with fury and she gave Layla a hard shove. Caught off-guard, Layla teetered for a moment before she fell back against the banister, hitting her head and back against the solid wood. Wincing, she straightened up, glaring at the other girl and battling the urge to retaliate and push her right back.

"If you ever lay a hand on me again," she snapped, "you'll regret it."

With a sneer on her lips, Hala disappeared down the hallway. Tears pricked Layla's eyes as she rubbed the back of her head. She had done nothing to deserve the other girl's enmity and the unfairness of her attack stung. As she blinked the tears away, Layla realized the pin that held her gray scarf together must have dropped off when she hit the banister. She could now feel her exposed hair.

The next moment, she heard footsteps coming up the stairs. Not wishing to be discovered in tears and with her hair showing, she ran into the hallway opposite the one Hala had taken. Coming to a door at the end, she turned the knob and peered cautiously into a sitting room. It was empty and quiet. She entered and closed the door, wiping the tears with the end of her scarf before wrapping the fabric as best as she could around her head. She froze as she heard footsteps coming towards the suite she was hiding in.

In a panic, she ducked behind a large sofa, hugging her arms around her as the door opened and someone came and sat down on the sofa. She almost gasped in dismay when she heard Faisal speaking into a cell phone. She had unwittingly placed herself in the position of eavesdropper. Now, she could not very well walk away without embarrassing them both. Shrinking into a miserable ball of mortification, she tried not to listen to what he was saying but it was impossible.

"Of course, I understand," Faisal was saying. "I know there's no turning back. I made a commitment and I'm sticking with it." There was a minute of silence as he listened to the person at the other end. Then he gave a harsh laugh and said, "I'm certainly not getting cold feet. Yes, yes, I know it's not going to be easy. I promise you I'll do whatever it takes, no matter the cost. You can count on me."

With that note of finality in his voice, he ended the call and Layla heard him striding over to the bedchamber beyond. Seeing her chance, she got to her feet and crept over to the door. Moments later, she was flying down the stairs. Her ire with Hala was now replaced by a sudden chill. There had been an ominous quality to Faisal's words. Was he one of *Al-Aqrab's* accomplices?

Chapter Fifteen
A Trying Time

THE TEENAGERS MET before lunch in Adam's suite to compare notes. In order for Layla to report on her encounter with Hala and subsequent flight to Faisal's room, she had to tell the boys of her very first run-in with the girl on the night of Jumana's arrival. Predictably, they were outraged.

"You have to tell her father," said Adam. "Otherwise, she'll continue her spiteful behavior."

"It will make things worse," said Layla. "And she won't listen to him anyway."

"Then you should tell Tariq," said Zahra. "I think she'll pay attention to him. You can tell him she made a nasty remark and when you replied, she pushed you against the banister. You don't have to tell him all the details."

"Okay," Layla agreed reluctantly.

She went on to tell them about Faisal's phone conversation.

"It sounds suspicious," said Adam. "In fact, he's a strong suspect as *Al-Aqrab's* accomplice. If Tariq's out of the way, Faisal stands to get a larger inheritance from the Shaykh."

"Yes, it would have been easy for him to put the stone in Tariq's saddle and plant the scorpion on Tariq's bed," said Zaid. "You have to tell Tariq what you heard, Layla."

"He might be upset we suspect his family," said Layla.

"He needs to know everything we see and hear," said Adam. "His life is at stake here."

"It's a good thing Faisal didn't see you in his room, Layla," said Zahra. "That would have been embarrassing."

"You can say that again," said Layla. "Oh, and one more thing. I found shoe prints by the window where the Woman in White was standing the night we came. She must have known we were coming and wanted to make sure we saw her."

Zahra gave her report next. "Two women in black face veils came together into the forecourt. They took the path around the side of the castle to the kitchen, so I guessed they were kitchen staff. After them came three men who went in the direction of the stables. Next came a meat delivery van which drove around to the kitchen and left fifteen minutes later. No one else came or left while I was there."

"I suppose the staff and delivery people are given the security code to punch in at the gate," said Zaid. "But still, if someone with evil intention wants to get into the castle, they could get the code from an accomplice."

"Or they could be let in from the postern gate," said Adam. "I found it locked from the inside by a big bolt. When I opened it, there was not much to see except more trees and undergrowth outside. For all we know, both the Cloaked Man and the Woman in White could be coming from Khaldun through that gate."

When it was Zaid's turn to give his report, he said, "I didn't notice anything out of the ordinary at the stables. The staff was busy with their work. A few of them spoke to each other in *Domari* so I knew they were gypsy. Now for the strange part. When I was coming back, I saw our maid, Nura, heading towards the lookout tower. Curious, I followed her and saw her standing on the path, staring up at the tower. When she saw me, she hurried back to the castle. I decided to go up and look around. When I got there, the smell of incense was strong. I found some ashes in the fireplace."

"I wonder if Nura is the one burning the incense sticks," said Zahra. "Some superstitious people believe it chases away bad energy or something of the sort."

"Maybe she thinks it will chase away the evil that is waiting and watching around us," said Layla. "Now that we've found out about *Al-Aqrab*, there's probably some truth to what she said."

"I think she's just superstitious," said Adam. "Let's continue to keep our eyes open. Hopefully, we'll find out something soon."

LUNCH WAS NOT a comfortable meal for Layla. She could feel Hala's hateful gaze on her several times. It was hard to keep a pleasant expression on her face when she felt like baring her teeth at the other girl. As for Faisal, Layla found herself studying him and wondering about the conversation she had overheard. *Would he commit murder, so he could get a larger bequest?* He could be unpleasant sometimes but that didn't make him murderer material. And even though he was the most likely suspect, it didn't eliminate the other cousins from being suspects too.

WHEN THEY ARRIVED at the stables at two, Tariq was leaning against a storage shed, speaking with Raj, the Indian groom. After the dusky-skinned man left, Tariq said, "Raj told me they're a bit short-handed in the stables today. We'll have to wait a few minutes for the horses to be ready."

"Did the head groom say anything about that stone under your saddle?" asked Adam.

"Yes, Hatem spoke to Kamal, the groom who saddled Jasim. Kamal swore there was no stone when he saddled Jasim and if there had been one, he would have removed it. I believe him. He's been here for almost ten years and I know he's trustworthy. I have to accept that someone did put that stone under the saddle."

"Of course," Zaid could not resist saying. "I had no doubts about that."

"Hatem told me Raj will be checking the horses from now on," said Tariq. "It's just hard to accept that anyone would wish to harm me."

Adam cast an eye around. Seeing no one nearby, he said, "Tariq, we've been keeping an eye around the castle. Layla heard a suspicious conversation today in Faisal's room. But first, she'll have to tell you how it came about."

As she saw Tariq's puzzled expression, Layla regretted telling the others what had happened. She hated putting the youth at odds with his own family. But it was too late to retract any of it now. Sighing inwardly, she related her clash with Hala, careful to leave Tariq's name out of it.

When she was finished, Tariq's face was thunderous. "I will talk to Hala. Sometimes she goes too far."

Layla then told him what she had overhead in Faisal's room.

Tariq looked troubled now. "What Faisal said sounds suspicious. But I can't believe any of my family would be in league with such a dangerous man as *Al-Aqrab*. There must be others here who are *Al-Aqrab's* accomplices."

They heard soft footsteps and Hatem came around the corner of the shed, a strange, shuttered look on his face. Without a word, he walked past them to his office.

They all stared after the head groom.

"Do you think he heard what we said?" asked Zahra.

"Yes, he had a weird look on his face," said Adam. "Like he was shocked to hear us talking about *Al-Aqrab.*"

"I think I've heard enough about *Al-Aqrab* to last me a lifetime," said Tariq. "Ah, here are our horses at last. Let's go enjoy our ride and forget our woes for a while."

Layla enjoyed the ride to the foothills that afternoon. There was no distressing incident to mar their pleasure this time and her confidence grew as she guided Ayah along the sandy trail. The wind whooshing against her face and the symphony of the horses' hooves clip-clopping on the ground filled her with a sense of wellbeing. Casting aside the worries of that day, she gave herself over to the sheer joy of the ride.

THEY WERE IN the inner courtyard, returning to the castle when they ran into no other than Hala. She was coming out of the recreation area, wearing a bulky blue robe, her hair dripping wet and a towel in her hand.

"Hala," Tariq called out. "I want to talk to you."

"What for?" she came to a stop, her face wary, as if she suspected what was in store.

Layla cringed. *Oh no. Surely Tariq's not going to tell Hala off in front of us?*

But Tariq did just that. "Why did you shove Layla on the stairway?"

Giving Layla a venomous look, Hala said, "I have no idea what lies she told you, Tariq. She had no business prying in our private family suites. And it wasn't my fault she was clumsy and fell down the stairs."

Layla's mouth opened in shock. Then she saw red. Unable to

keep her cool in the face of such an accusation and blatant lies to boot, she said, "Oh. My. God. You're such a liar. I told you I went to the third floor to explore. And I didn't fall down the stairs. You pushed me against the banister."

"Stop lying. You've been trying to cause trouble ever since you came here."

"No, you're the one who's lying and trying to cause trouble."

"Everything was fine until you came."

"You're the one who's been making snide remarks to me."

"If you don't like it, why don't you just leave?"

"I'll leave when I'm supposed to leave."

Caught in the crossfire between the two girls, Tariq looked out of his depth. "Hala, stop it. Control your temper and be nice to our guests."

"Why are you taking her side? I'm your family, not her. You should be telling her off, not me."

"You're the one at fault here, not Layla."

"She's got you twisted around her little finger." Hala's voice was bitter. "And you're too stupid to see it."

Tariq looked stunned. Color flooded his face and he looked embarrassed. Then anger set in. "You're out of line, Hala. If you can't control your tongue, keep out of our way."

"I hate you," Hala spat out on a sob. "And I hate her. I wish she'd never come here."

Chapter Sixteen
Discovery in the Dungeon

"I'M SORRY," SAID Tariq after Hala ran off. "I don't know what's wrong with her. Maybe I should ask Uncle Miftah to talk to her."

Layla shared a look with the others. Hala was jealous and Tariq had no clue.

She said, "No, it's okay. I think Hala's feeling left out because you're spending so much time with us."

"Then what's to stop her from joining us?"

"I don't know."

Truly, I don't know. If the girl spent time with us, all her silly thoughts of me and Tariq would go away.

"Are you still going to show us that special place you mentioned, Tariq?" asked Zaid.

"Yes. But have your refreshments first. Then meet me here in an hour."

TARIQ WAS WAITING for them in the inner courtyard, a knapsack in his hand. He took them to a door in the servants' wing. A flight of stairs led down to a formidable iron door.

"Welcome to the dungeon," he said.

"The dungeon," Layla exclaimed. "We didn't even know there was one."

"That's cool," said Adam.

"I can't wait to see it," said Zaid.

Zahra was the only one who did not look excited at the thought of seeing the mysterious underbelly of the castle. "I'm not too fond of underground places but I guess I'll come along."

Opening the knapsack, Tariq handed them each a flashlight.

"Isn't there electricity there?" asked Adam.

"No, Grandfather didn't think it was necessary since the dungeon is not being used. When sightseers come to the castle, it gives them a thrill to find it so dark."

Unlocking the two bolts on the iron door, they entered a square chamber.

"This used to be the guardroom when the dungeon was used as a prison," said Tariq. "The first set of prisoners were said to be anarchists who staged a coup against the sultan at that time."

Beyond the guardroom were a series of corridors which housed the prison cells. The ceiling, walls, and floors were fashioned of the same basalt rocks as the castle. The air was cooler and had the stale, musty smell of being trapped for ages in the same place. Surrounding the prison cells were several labyrinthine tunnels.

"The Sultan who built the castle had these tunnels dug as escape routes," said Tariq. "When the dungeon became a prison, the reigning sultan had all the escape routes closed up."

They walked along the corridors, shining their flashlights into the empty cells before setting forth into one of the tunnels. It was narrow and winding, the surfaces constructed of the same material as the cells. After walking a little way inside, they turned back and retraced their steps to the entrance.

Tariq shone the flashlight ahead. "I thought we left the door open."

"We did," said Zaid.

"It looks like it's locked now," said Layla.

A swift push verified that the door was indeed locked.

"I can't believe someone locked us inside," said Tariq.

"Maybe they didn't realize we were down here," said Adam.

"The door was wide open. They had to know someone was inside," was Tariq's grim reply.

"Do you think Hala could have done it out of spite?" asked Layla.

"I can't believe she would sink so low," said Tariq.

"It must be one of *Al-Aqrab's* accomplices," said Zahra.

"Let's kick the door," said Adam. "Maybe the bolts will break off."

The youths converged on the door and began kicking it. Next, they threw their weights against it but there was no budging it.

"What do we do now?" asked Zaid.

"We'll have to wait until someone realizes we're missing and comes looking for us," said Tariq.

"You think they'll look down here?" asked Adam

"I'm sure they will," said Tariq.

Layla hoped so. The thought of waiting for hours to be rescued filled her with dread.

"They won't know we're missing until dinner," said Zahra. "And that's almost three hours away." Her voice was filled with panic.

Layla laid a reassuring hand on her friend's shoulder. "I think we should explore the tunnels in the meantime. It will help to pass the time."

"That's a good idea," Zaid agreed.

"I'm game," said Adam.

"All right," said Tariq, "We'll explore the same one we went into just now."

They had not gone very far inside when they found the ceiling had caved-in. The second tunnel they tried had a caved-in floor. In the third tunnel, they had walked for about twenty minutes when it took on a more rough-hewn appearance. The basalt surfaces gave way to earthen ones, with thick snake-like spirals protruding from the ceilings.

"What are those things?" Zahra eyed the spirals with nervous eyes. "They look like snakes."

Tariq poked one of the spirals with his flashlight. It remained unmoving.

"Just as I thought," he said. "They're tree roots running underground."

Ten minutes later, they saw a long shaft of light ahead and became excited. To their disappointment they had come to the end of the tunnel. The light came from the queer funnel-shaped ceiling above. Through the long, narrow spire, daylight had sneaked in like a silent serpent.

"If only we could climb through that opening and escape," said Zahra.

"We'll need wings to get up there," said Layla.

"Or a ladder to climb up," said Zaid. As he moved forward, he tripped on the uneven ground and fell against Tariq. The two youths slammed into the wall with a dull thud, causing it to vibrate.

"Tariq, I'm sorry," Zaid exclaimed. "Are you okay?"

"Yes, I'm fine," said Tariq. "No harm done."

As the vibrations faded away, a rustling sound came to their ears. Layla stared up, wondering what stirred in the dark reaches of the funneled ceiling.

As Tariq shone the flashlight upwards, there came a screeching, rushing noise.

"Bats," Tariq gasped out. "Get down on the ground."

Crouching low, they covered their faces with their arms as the sounds of the flitting bats eddied around them. Layla tried not to think of the stories she had heard of vampire bats sucking the blood dry from one's body. She grimaced at the funky, moldy odor that came to her nostrils. *Ugh. We're probably wallowing in bat droppings.* She was relieved when the sounds ebbed away, leaving an eerie silence.

"I was right about needing wings to get up there," she whispered.

"The bats must have become disturbed when we hit the wall," said Zaid. "I've never seen so many of them before."

"Let's crawl away so we don't disturb them again," said Adam.

"Wait, I feel something on the wall where we tripped," Tariq whispered, shining his flashlight on the spot. The light fell upon a long, rusty brass handle protruding from the wall. It was attached to a square indentation. "It looks like a door. I wonder if it's one of the Sultan's escape routes. Maybe he didn't close them all up."

"He could have left one as a bolt hole in case of an emergency," said Adam.

"Let's open it and see," said Layla, impatient to know what lay beyond the door.

While the girls aimed their flashlights at the handle, the three youths yanked on it. After several tries, the square door opened with a grating sound to reveal an aperture in the wall. Behind it was an empty, craggy space.

"It looks like more tunnels back there," said Zaid. "Let's check it out."

They went through the aperture and into a rough cave that looked like it had been carved out by a giant fist.

"I think we're in the caves under the Dukhan Hills." Tariq's voice echoed as he moved the flashlight in a circular motion in front of him. "There's a whole bunch of them resembling honeycombs. Uncle Rashid liked coming here to explore. He brought me a few times. Spelunkers come often and tourists once in a while."

"Who are spelunkers?" asked Zahra.

"They're people who makes a hobby of exploring and studying caves."

"Dad would love it here," said Zaid. "He went once to the *Majlis al Jinn* cave in Oman and had a great time there."

"The Meeting Place of the *Jinn*," said Layla. "What a fitting name for a cave. Hmm, there must be a couple of friendly neighborhood *jinns* around here too."

"It looks like a maze," said Adam. "It's a pity we don't have any string, or we'd use it to come back here if we get lost. You think we'll be able to find our way out, Tariq?"

"We should be able to, *insha Allah.* There are several openings that lead out. If not, there's a great cave in the middle where Uncle Rashid brought me a few times. If we could find it, I know the way out from there. We'll go in a straight line and see what happens. Follow behind me and don't step out of line. The caves are filled with deep pits and shafts that you won't notice until you fall into one. Ready?"

"Yes," they replied.

They moved forward, giving the depressed areas of earth a wide berth. One cave turned to another and Layla was beginning to think they were going around in circles when they came to an enormous cave. Stalactites, some long and spindly and others thick and conical, hung from the ceiling. They glowed in the reflection from the flashlights, filling the cave with a ghostly glow. The walls were jagged hunks of rocks and the ground filled with many hollows and dips. It was a beautiful place with an alien, otherworldly feel to it.

It feels like we're on a distant galaxy or the set of a science fiction movie.

"This is the great cave I was telling you about," said Tariq. "I know how to get out from here."

"That's great," said Zahra. "I was beginning to think we'd never find our way out."

"It's so beautiful and peaceful here," said Zaid. "It makes me think of the Companions of the Cave story in the *Qur'an*. The youths and their dog must have slept in a cave just like this one."

"They're also known as the Sleepers of Ephesus," said Adam. "Imagine waking up after such a long time and finding a different world."

From the great cave, Tariq led them on a straight course until they saw the unmistakable shine of daylight ahead. Excited now, they ran out of the opening. They emerged onto a rocky tract with towering gray hills and slanting rays of sunlight streaming from above.

Tariq laughed joyfully. "Welcome to the Dukhan Hills."

"Oh, I'm so glad we escaped from the dungeon," cried Zahra.

Chapter Seventeen
The Woman in White

DESPITE HAVING TO walk back to the castle after their arduous trek through the dungeon and caves, the teenagers were jubilant. They had found an escape route from the dark bowels of the castle. It gave them a sense of satisfaction to think they had outwitted their unknown enemy and emerged the victors of that skirmish.

"Let's not tell anyone about our discovery," said Tariq. "Let whoever locked us in wonder how we escaped."

He kept them entertained with local Khaldunian legends of the Nawaf Desert as they trudged back to the castle.

"I'd like to see the desert," said Adam. "Especially the spot where Rashid fell."

The others endorsed the idea and Tariq agreed to take them there the following afternoon.

"We'll take the horses," he said. "It will be good practice for you."

They returned to the castle via the gate in the paddock. The first person they saw was Hatem. The head groom looked startled to see them. *I wonder if he had a hand in locking us in the dungeon?* Layla waved cheekily at him for good measure and he inclined his head as they passed by. When they entered the inner courtyard and checked the door of the dungeon, they found it open.

"What a mean trick," said Tariq. "Whoever locked it has opened it now."

"Well, we have the last laugh," said Zaid. "If they wanted to frighten us, they failed."

AFTER A REFRESHING bath, Layla donned a floral aqua dress with a matching scarf and followed the others down to dinner. As they ate, she was surprised to hear Ghazala speaking in a hoarse voice. The older woman was wearing dark colors which only emphasized the peaky look of her face, the red tip of her nose, and the feverish brightness of her eyes.

"Whatever happened to your voice, Ghazzy?" asked Suha.

"It's the air conditioning," Ghazala croaked. "It's given me a cold."

Had she lost her voice because of the air conditioning or had she lost it from screaming last night? Could she be the Woman in White?

Layla voiced her suspicion to the others later when they met up in Zahra's suite.

"It could be any of the women, except for Jumana, Suha and Hala," said Zaid. "That leaves Auntie Ghazala, Mrs. Haddad, the female servants or some unknown woman from Khaldun."

Adam said, "I can't see Auntie Ghazala doing it and I don't see why Mrs. Haddad would do it either. It must be one of the servants or a woman from Khaldun."

"It could even be our maid, Nura," said Layla. "She's certainly been acting suspicious, talking of evil and staring at the tower."

"What if the ghoul plans to come back tonight?" said Zahra.

"We could lay in wait for her and be right there on the spot to catch her."

"I like that idea," said Adam. "It might be a waste of time if she doesn't show up but I'm willing to take that chance."

"It's fine with me," said Zaid.

"Me too," said Layla.

"Since she shows up around midnight, let's set our clocks to wake at eleven forty," said Adam. "We should be hiding in the grove before twelve strikes."

"I don't think I'll be able to sleep a wink," said Layla.

JUST BEFORE TWELVE, the teenagers took their positions in the grove, squatting behind the thick undergrowth and hoping they would not have long to wait. A crescent moon with glowing corona hung like a centerpiece from a sky festooned with a smattering of stars. The chirping of cicadas and the far-off howl of a jackal were the only sounds to be heard. The shadows of the trees swathed them in a safe cloak of darkness and the muggy night air was like warm breath on their cheeks.

"Let's hope we're in luck tonight," Zaid murmured. "I really hated getting out of bed."

"You can say that again," said Layla. Contrary to her declaration of not being able to sleep a wink, she had fallen asleep within minutes of her head hitting the pillow. She had credited their foray into the dungeon for her tiredness. Her eyes still felt a bit gritty though the night air had dispelled most of her grogginess.

Layla shifted position, only to freeze when the sound of rustling foliage and the shuffling of feet came to their ears. They peeked through the undergrowth as someone emerged from the trees. But it was not the Woman in White. It was the Cloaked

Man again. He was coming from the back of the grove and heading towards the inner courtyard. The darkness coupled with his voluminous dark cloak made it difficult to identify him.

At a silent signal from Adam, they began to follow the cloaked figure. Through the trees and towards the arcade they kept him within sight until he came to the inner courtyard. Taking cover under an olive tree, they watched as he crossed the courtyard and headed to the servant quarters. He opened one of the doors with a key and stepped inside. As he turned in their direction to lock the door, the light of the lantern fell upon his scarred face.

"Hatem," Zahra breathed out. "He's the Cloaked Man."

Above the murmur of the water fountain, they heard mewing and watched as Bilqis came slinking across the courtyard. The gleam from a lantern reflected off her eyes, turning them into glowing balls of fire. She came to a stop, her head up as she sniffed the air. She began to stalk towards one of the terra cotta urns. A small jerboa darted out from behind it and ran for dear life towards the orchard. With a ferocious snarl, Bilqis dashed after it, a silver-white streak of quivering fur. A figure at the back of the courtyard gave a muffled shriek as jerboa and cat ran past.

"The Woman in White," Layla exclaimed. "There she is."

"Come on, after her," said Adam.

As they ran towards her, the Woman in White turned her head and saw them. Picking up her gown, she took to her heels and raced towards the orchard. They pelted down the courtyard after her. She was almost at the edge of the dark wall of trees. The next moment, she stumbled and went sprawling to the ground.

"We've got her," Layla cried. Even as she spoke, the Woman in White scrambled to her feet and disappeared into the trees. One moment she was there and the next she was gone. After several minutes of searching, there was no sign of her.

"She must have taken off her white clothes, so she could

hide in the darkness," said Zaid. "We'd better go back. We can't outwait her."

"We were so close to getting her," Zahra lamented. "Just a few more seconds and we would have caught her."

Bitterly disappointed, they conceded defeat and returned to bed.

ALONE WITH TARIQ at breakfast the next morning, they took turns telling him in hushed tones of their adventure last night. Jumana entered and Layla noticed at once that the older woman was walking with a slight limp. An image of the Woman in White tripping on the ground last night came to her mind. But no, Jumana could not be the Woman in White. The fake ghoul had been around before Jumana came on the scene. All the same, it seemed suspicious that she should be limping after the Woman in White fell last night.

Chapter Eighteen
In the Nawaf Desert

For THEIR TRIP to the Nawaf Desert that afternoon, they wore comfortable riding gear and each of them carried a water bottle. Besides their safety helmets, they also wore dark sunglasses. Tariq had requested a picnic from the kitchen. It had come packed in a huge knapsack. At the paddock, they found Raj waiting with their horses and Hatem tending to a horse nearby.

The head groom's gaze swept over them, lingering on their water bottles and the knapsack Tariq was hitching to the saddle. *I wonder what Hatem is up to, creeping about in the night. I can see him being Al-Aqrab's accomplice with his watchful eyes.*

Tariq had warned them it was going to be quite a ride to the desert. Layla was prepared for the brisk pace they set off at. Ayah's body was comfortable and familiar now. As Layla spurred the mare into a canter, she felt a warm rush of affection for the docile animal. The sun was strong and fierce, but a refreshing breeze whipped at their faces and tore at their clothes. After several miles of riding, Layla knew they had left the oasis behind as the terrain began to look gray and desolate. By the time they reached the desert, Layla's back was plastered with sweat and her mouth dry from the heat. They paused for a few minutes to swig at their water bottles and rest the horses before setting off again.

The Nawaf Desert stretched for miles before them, a barren sea of unrelenting sand and dancing mirages. High above, a pack of vultures circled in the air, on the lookout for carcasses to scavenge upon. From what Tariq had told them, Layla knew the desert was considered to be as unpredictable as a frivolous child. The Bedouins had been the foremost in promoting tales of strange happenings. It had given the desert an aura of mystique. She clutched at Ayah's reins as an angry gust of wind kicked up sand around them. Tariq had told them the summer *shamal* which caused sandstorms had ended in early July. *But a stray one could head our way, couldn't it?*

"What's that funnel-like formation going up in the air, Tariq?" asked Adam.

"Oh, it's just a dust devil. Nothing to be afraid of."

"I don't trust anything that's named after the devil," said Layla, eyeing the sandy funnel with wary eyes.

Tariq slowed down as they approached a section of moistened sand.

"It's a camel wallow," he told them. "Camels come and thrash around in the sand, making it watery and loose enough to get stuck in. We've got to go around it." Skirting around the camel wallow, Layla patted Ayah's back as they gained solid ground again.

The curved shapes of sand dunes appeared on the horizon.

"We're coming close to the Dunes of the Devil," said Tariq.

"What, they're named after the devil too?" asked Layla.

Tariq laughed. "I'm afraid so. *Ta'al.* Come, you'll soon see why the Bedouins gave them such a nickname."

They set off at a slow gallop until the Dunes of the Devil rose in curvy crests before them, rippling formations of mountainous sand that filled them with awe. They were still some distance away when they heard a strange but melodic booming, whistling sound. As they approached the base of the dunes and reined in their horses, the sound became louder.

"Where's that noise coming from?" Zahra's head swiveled around.

"From the sand dunes," Zaid exclaimed. "They're singing sand dunes. I remember reading there were some in the Nawaf Desert."

"Wow, the dunes actually make that sound?" asked Adam.

"Yes," said Tariq. "Before modern physics explained the reason for this phenomenon— that the sounds were actually caused by the friction of the sand grains—the Bedouins believed evil *jinns* lived in them. That's why they called them the Dunes of the Devil."

"It's a fitting name," said Adam. "Anyone hearing such a racket for the first time would think it the work of the devil himself."

They stood for a few minutes listening to the song of the dunes before setting off again. The sand shifted around them, as if prodded by unseen fingers. Tariq halted again for them to drink more water and rest the horses.

Zaid, who had turned to look towards the dunes, said, "There's a man on horseback by the dunes. I think he's watching us."

The others turned around and saw the man sitting motionless on his horse, looking in their direction. He must have realized they were watching him for he turned and disappeared behind one of the dunes.

"I hope he's not one of *Al-Aqrab's* accomplices come to finish us off," said Zahra.

"He looks like a nomad herdsman," said Tariq. "As long as he keeps his distance, we don't have anything to worry about."

They resumed their journey and the solid outline of a range began to dominate the horizon.

"That's the Gurian Plateau," said Tariq. "We're approaching Gurian Valley."

The ground began to dip downwards. The sea of sand gave way to green tracts of vegetation, revealing a well-worn pathway that wound downwards into the valley. Layla braced back in the saddle, digging her heels in the stirrup as they continued slowly down the slope.

Gurian Valley was spread out in green splendor before them, a hidden jewel in a harsh landscape. Fed by rain water from the plateau, it was abundant with gnarled juniper trees, acacias, and barberry shrubs. In the center stood a small lake ringed by wild grass and reeds. At their arrival, a flock of birds flew off with startled screeches.

"Those are white-collared kingfishers," said Tariq. "This lake is a popular watering hole for humans, birds, and beasts alike."

Following him, they led the horses to the lake and let them drink of the water. After the animals had drunk their fill, they were hitched to the juniper trees, where they contented themselves by cropping at the leaves within reach. On foot, the teenagers made their way up the rocky plateau, until they reached the rock-strewn top. The land leveled out in front of them for several yards before dipping down into the Gurian Ravine with a stomach-churning drop. Mindful of what had befallen Tariq's uncle, they were careful not to go any further. Layla clung to a huge boulder as she stared in awe at the rugged beauty of the mist-enshrouded ranges. She felt as insignificant as a speck of dirt in comparison to their gargantuan proportions.

"Uncle Rashid fell from somewhere along this point," said Tariq. "They couldn't pinpoint the exact location."

They stood in somber silence for a few minutes. Afterwards, they returned to the valley and began their picnic under the shade of an acacia tree. In the knapsack were *shawarma* beef sandwiches and lamb *kibbeh* patties. For dessert, there was fruit cake and fresh slices of pineapple. To quench their thirst were bottles of water and mango juice.

Layla noticed Tariq had a pouch slung around his neck. She stared at it, wondering what it held. Her brother must have had the same thought for he asked, "What's in that pouch, Tariq? Anything special?"

"Let me show you." Opening the pouch, he pulled out two sheathed knives. "These are for protection. No one comes to the desert without a rifle or hunting knives. You never know when you might run into a hostile animal."

They sat in a circle as they ate, shaded from the full heat of the sun.

"Rashid looked a lot like Faisal, didn't he, Tariq?" asked Layla, as she munched on her sandwich. "I came across his portrait in the gallery when I was exploring the third floor."

"*Na'am.* Yes, they shared a certain resemblance though they were different in temperament. Uncle Rashid was patient and level-headed while Faisal...well, you know how he is."

"Has Faisal always been like that?" asked Layla.

"No, he used to be a lot more pleasant. After he and his wife separated, he turned into this moody, malicious person."

"He was married?" Zahra's eyes opened wide.

"Yes, two years ago. He and Naeema were together for only six months before they went their separate ways. Faisal acts like it never happened and hates anyone bringing it up. Grandfather was hoping Faisal and Naeema would get back together since they haven't divorced but that doesn't seem likely. They were happy at the beginning, but no one knows what went wrong."

After they had eaten, they packed the remains of their picnic into the knapsack. They were washing their hands in the lake when Zahra reached out among the stones at the shallow end and fished out something from the water.

"Look what I found," she said.

They stared at the object in her hand. It was a wristwatch, waterlogged and a bit rusty from its sojourn in the lake.

"Let me see it," said Tariq.

He took it from Zahra and examined it. Then he looked at them with pain-filled eyes. "It was Uncle Rashid's watch."

Chapter Nineteen

Jumana's Secret

"**R**EALLY?" SAID LAYLA.

"Yes, I had it custom-made for him last *Eid*. Look." He pointed to a tiny inscription in the back. It read, *To Uncle Rashid, from Tariq*.

"I wonder how it got into the lake," said Adam.

"I don't know," said Tariq. "But I'm convinced more than ever that Uncle Rashid was murdered."

THE NEXT MORNING, after breakfast and a short swim, the teenagers decided to stake out the castle again. This time, Adam opted for the stables, Zaid the forecourt, Zahra inside the castle and Layla the inner courtyard. They arranged to meet in Zaid's suite before lunch to compare notes again. In the courtyard, Layla slouched down on a wicker chair under one of the olive trees, concealed behind a giant urn of flowers. The day was steamy and humid, the heat seeming to drain all the energy from her body. *I don't think I'll be able to stay outside for long.*

She observed the comings and goings of the castle's servants. *How like busy bees they are, flitting about their hive.* She watched with interest as Qais, Shaykh Sulaiman's nurse, strolled out and seated himself under an olive tree on the opposite side of the courtyard. He must have come out for some fresh air and sunlight. The only times they ever saw him was in Shaykh Sulaiman's suite or in the gym. They had also ran into Dr. Hakam, the Shaykh's doctor, twice in the Shaykh's suite.

Ten minutes later, Qais stood up and headed back into the castle. For such a hefty man, he was surprisingly quiet on his feet. As she stared at his retreating back, Layla could not help thinking what a misfit he seemed as a nurse with his wide shoulders and massive hands. His size was useful for helping Shaykh Sulaiman with therapy, but Qais still seemed like an unknown quantity. Was he just a simple nurse, or was there more to him than met the eye?

She was still pondering that question when Jumana came striding out into the courtyard. The older woman was wearing a midnight-blue dress with a light-blue scarf, and a pair of sensible shoes. There was no trace of the limp from yesterday. Her face bore a reflective expression, as if her mind was preoccupied with some grave matter. She did not notice Layla under the olive tree. She was walking towards the orchard.

Should I follow her? Maybe I could pump her for information about her argument with Rashid. Now is the perfect time to tackle her. As Jumana neared the orchard, Layla got to her feet and strode towards the green wall of trees. Once she was among the trees, Layla trod quietly. It was much cooler under the shady branches and she listened with pleasure to the chirping of birds as she strolled along. She saw a flash of blue ahead and knew she was on the right track.

Jumana walked all the way to the Garden of Dreams and sat on one of the white stone benches under the cypresses. Concealed behind a fragrant clump of blooming white jasmine,

Layla had a clear view of her. She watched as Jumana took out a letter from her pocket and began to read. It must have been a short letter for only moments later she tucked it back into her pocket. Then she covered her face with the palms of her hands and bowed over as if in pain.

It took Layla a few moments to realize that Jumana was crying, her body shaking with silent sobs. Layla stared in dismay at the weeping woman. She knew it was an invasion of privacy to watch Jumana. She just could not bring herself to leave. There was some mystery here and she meant to find out what it was.

When Jumana finally sat up and dabbed at her eyes with the tail of her scarf, Layla walked towards her. "Hello, Jumana."

Jumana looked startled. "Oh Layla, it's you."

"Feeling better?"

Jumana looked embarrassed. "I guess you saw me wallowing in self-pity."

"I'm sorry to disturb you, but are you okay?"

"I'm fine. I just needed to get some things out of my system."

"And have you gotten them out?"

Jumana stared unseeingly at the beautiful roses. "I don't know. Only time will tell."

"You were crying about Rashid, weren't you?"

Jumana stared now at the engagement ring on her finger. "Yes."

"You loved him very much, didn't you?"

"I thought we were soulmates. I felt I was the most blessed woman on earth when we got engaged. But then it all started to go wrong."

"How did it go wrong?"

Jumana sighed. "It's a long story. And you're too young to hear my troubles."

"Try me," said Layla. "I've been told I'm very mature for my age. People think I'm older than I am."

Jumana gave a watery smile. "What, they think you're thirteen when you're twelve?"

"I'm fourteen." Layla's voice was indignant. "But I could pass for sixteen."

"Still too young. Besides, it's complicated. You wouldn't understand."

"I read a lot and have a good head for language," said Layla. "If I can understand Shakespeare, methinks perchance I wilt understand thou."

Jumana gave a reluctant chuckle. "You're a very persuasive young lady. Maybe it will help if I talk to you. I couldn't bring myself to tell my family. Neither could I confide in anyone here. If I tell you my story, you have to promise not to tell anyone."

Layla concealed her smile of triumph. "I promise I won't tell anyone."

"Come, sit here." Jumana patted the space next to her. After Layla sat down, Jumana said, "The nightmare began with the theft of my bracelet and the suicide of Tariq's tutor."

"Yes, Tariq told us about that."

"It was a horrid shock, as you can imagine. Especially Lamis's claim that Rashid had broken his promise to marry her. I knew it wasn't true, but as the weeks passed by, I began to notice a change in Rashid. He seemed ill at ease when I came to the castle. As our wedding came nearer, he was so distant and distracted that I was ensnared by the evil whisperer. I started to think that maybe Lamis had told the truth in that letter. Maybe Rashid had wanted to marry her and Uncle Sulaiman didn't approve."

"Tariq told us Rashid had eyes for only you," said Layla.

"Believe me, I was ashamed of those thoughts and tried my best to chase them away. But on my last visit here, a few days before Rashid died and five weeks before our wedding, he asked me to meet him in the courtyard. When I came, he told me he wished to delay the wedding. After I got over the shock, I asked him why. He said he needed more time. That was the last straw.

I told him it was obvious he no longer wanted to marry me and to consider our engagement broken."

Jumana's eyes filled with tears again and she dabbed at them with her scarf.

"That's the argument you had in the courtyard?"

"Yes, the servants are too observant."

"What happened after you told Rashid you were breaking the engagement?"

"He told me not to make any hasty decisions, that all he wanted was more time. I told him I would give him ten days. After that time, he would either agree to the appointed wedding date or tell me the real reason why he wanted to delay it. If he did neither, then I would announce our engagement was broken."

"What did he say to that?"

"From his face, I could see the struggle going on inside him. In the end he agreed, and we left the courtyard. I didn't see any point in remaining at the castle. I went back home the next day. Within a few days, we got news of his death. The strain was too much for me. I took to my bed, unable to come and console Uncle Sulaiman and the family. I feel a little better now. But I'm still in the dark why Rashid wanted to postpone our wedding. It's been bothering me ever since."

"You have no idea what it could be?"

"None at all. We would have been married by now had everything gone according to plan. But our faith teaches us not to speculate on what might or might not have been. I must face reality and move on. Come, we should go back now. It's becoming quite hot."

"Is your leg better now? I noticed you limping yesterday."

"I fell from my horse and banged my knee several years ago. I get little twinges now and then."

After she and Jumana parted ways, Layla went straight up to the cool comfort of her room. Grabbing a bottle of mango juice from the fridge, she flopped down on the sofa and contemplated what she had heard in the Garden of Dreams. Had Jumana spoken the truth? If so, why had Rashid wanted to delay the wedding? Was that what he had been telling Tariq that night? If it was, why hadn't he told Jumana?

Layla suddenly remembered the letter she had seen Jumana reading. The distraught woman had not made mention of it and Layla had quite forgotten about it during their conversation. Who had the letter been from? Had it been responsible for Jumana's storm of tears? Layla's instinct told her Jumana had been truthful. And genuinely heartbroken over Rashid's death. She could not have been involved.

Perhaps it had been a condolence letter? *It's a pity I couldn't tell her about Tariq's suspicion that Rashid was murdered. But we've promised him not to tell anyone. Now I'm bound by my promise not to reveal Jumana's secret. If Jumana and Tariq could only confide in each other, perhaps we'd get some answers.*

WHEN THEY MET in Zaid's suite before lunch, he was the only one who had something of interest to report.

"When I was returning from the stables, I decided to take a walk by the lookout tower. To my surprise, I saw our maid, Nura, coming up the pathway. I wondered if she had been up to the tower. After she was out of sight, I went up. There were fresh incense stick ashes in the fireplace. She has to be the one lighting them."

"She seems to have a fixation with the tower," said Adam.

"Maybe she is the Woman in White," said Zahra.

Layla felt guilty she was privy to information she could not share with the others. Throughout the afternoon, she tried to think of a way to get Tariq and Jumana to confide in each other, but to no avail. Little did she know her dilemma would be resolved that very evening and in the most unexpected way imaginable.

Chapter Twenty
The Hooded Horseman

THE TEENAGERS WERE playing a board game in Layla's suite that night when Tariq came by. The curly-haired youth was dressed in black and blue plaid pajamas. Layla felt a momentary twinge of fear. Had Tariq found another scorpion on his bed? But no, he seemed more thoughtful than terrified.

"You have something to tell us?" asked Adam.

"Yes. I remembered a bit more of what Uncle Rashid told me that night."

"You did?" said Zahra. "Go on, tell us. I can't bear the suspense."

"He told me someone had been sending him anonymous letters."

"Anonymous letters," Layla exclaimed. "About what?"

"I don't know. I don't think he told me. Or if he did, I don't remember that part."

"What made you remember it was anonymous letters?" asked Zaid.

"I was reading a book when all of a sudden it came to me."

"Maybe someone was blackmailing him and he found out who it was," said Adam. "And that's why he was murdered. The blackmailer could have hired *Al-Aqrab* to commit the murder."

"I can't think why anyone would blackmail Uncle Rashid," said Tariq. "He lived a quiet and useful life."

"Hopefully something will come to light soon," said Layla. "We'll be on the lookout."

After Tariq left, the teenagers continued their game. Fifteen minutes later, he was back, a frown of worry on his face.

"What's wrong?" asked Layla.

"Jumana seems to be missing."

"Missing?" said Adam. "How can that be?"

"When I went back to my suite, our butler Dhul Fikar, was talking to Aunt Ghazzy in the hallway. When I asked what happened, he said that at a quarter to nine, he saw Jum-Jum heading to the domed hall. She was wearing a shawl around her shoulders and it looked as if she was going outside. When she saw him, she told him to have the kitchen prepare a hot chocolate and send it up to her room at nine-thirty. At nine-thirty, Ramla, the maid who takes care of Jum-Jum's suite, took the hot chocolate up. When she came back down, she said Jum-Jum wasn't in her room, so she left the hot chocolate there. Dhul Fikar got worried, that's why he went to Aunt Ghazzy. I told them Jum-Jum's got to be around somewhere and we'll look for her."

"If she was going outside, maybe she went out with her car," said Zaid.

"Let's go look," said Adam.

When they got to the forecourt, Jumana's car was still there.

"If she didn't go with her car, where could she have gone?" asked Zahra.

"Let's go outside the gate and look around," said Layla

Minutes later, they were outside the gate. Layla's foot touched something soft. Stooping, she picked it up. "Look, it's a shawl. It must have been the one Jumana was wearing. She must have dropped it."

"Where could she be?" said Tariq in an anxious voice.

"Let's spread out and see if we can find her," said Zaid. "There's enough moonlight for us to see by."

They had just started off when Zahra gave a cry. "There she is. There's Jumana."

A feminine figure in long skirts came through the moonlight towards them. Layla recognized Jumana's short, graceful strides.

Tariq rushed to her. "Jum-Jum, what are you doing out here? We were so worried."

"I'm sorry." Jumana's voice was a thin thread. "I was very foolish to come outside."

"What happened?" asked Zahra.

"I was kidnapped."

"Kidnapped?!" they all cried out.

"Yes. Fortunately, I was rescued."

"Rescued? By whom?" asked Adam.

"By him," she said in a bemused voice as she turned around and pointed to a limestone hill. The teenagers stared with wide eyes and open mouths. Beneath the lambent light of a gibbous moon, a hooded man sat on a horse. He looked down at them for a long moment before he turned and vanished from sight.

"The Hooded Horseman," Tariq exclaimed. "You must tell us everything. I can't believe you were in such danger."

"What made you come look for me?"

"You were not in your room when Ramla took up the hot chocolate," said Tariq. "Dhul Fikar got worried and went to tell Aunt Ghazzy. I told them we'll find you."

"Ah, the hot chocolate," said Jumana. "Thank Allah for observant servants."

"You must tell us what happened," said Tariq.

"Alright, come to my room," said Jumana.

When they returned to the castle, Dhul Fikar looked relieved when he saw Jumana.

"Tell Ghazzy I'm fine, Dhul Fikar," said Jumana. "I just went out for a little while."

They followed her back to her suite to listen to her story. As she sipped on what had to be lukewarm chocolate, she told them she had received a letter from an unknown person that morning.

"It said: 'Come alone outside the gate at nine tonight. Have very important information about Rashid's death. Don't tell anyone or you'll learn nothing.' At the bottom it was signed, 'From a Well-Wisher.'"

The letter she was reading in the garden.

"When I got there," Jumana went on, "two men came out of the darkness and grabbed me. They put a gag over my mouth, tied my hands behind my back and blindfolded me. One of them picked me up and slung me up in front of him on a horse. I've never been so terrified in my life. I prayed to be saved from an evil fate. We had ridden for some time when I heard cries of surprise from the men. The one whose horse I rode on dismounted, and the sounds of a fight came to my ears. I felt frightened and helpless and hoped the horse wouldn't bolt. The fighting went on for about twenty minutes before everything went silent. Then someone came and untied my hands before removing my gag and blindfold."

"What did you see?" asked Zahra.

"In the darkness, I saw a man wearing a hood, with only his eyes showing. There was no sign of the two men who had tried to kidnap me. I guess they must have run away. The hooded man had fought them in order to rescue me. I didn't know how or why he came when he did but I thanked Allah. Then I thanked the hooded man."

"What happened after that?" said Layla.

"I turned the horse around and started to ride back to

the castle. He followed behind. When I came to that hill, I dismounted from the horse and left it there. The Hooded Man rode atop the hill so he could watch me walk back to safety. And here I am."

"The stories about him rescuing people are true," said Tariq. "We must let the police know about this kidnapping attempt. Those men must be caught."

"Oh, no," said Jumana. "I don't want anyone to know of my foolishness. It's absolutely mortifying."

Though he argued with her, Tariq could not shake her resolve.

"Did you see what those two men looked like?" asked Adam.

"No, it was too dark to make out their features. They spoke in Domari, so I knew they were gypsy. The only words I understood were Dukhan Hills. I guess they were planning to hide me in the caves there."

The young people stared at one another as the pieces fell into place.

"It's the message from the cipher," Zaid exclaimed. "Jumana was the bird to be caught, the gypsy men must be the catchers and the cage the Dukhan Hills."

"It's *Al-Aqrab's* work," Tariq burst out.

"What message are you talking about and what does a scorpion have to do with it?" said Jumana.

"It's a long story," said Tariq.

"I'm not going anywhere," said Jumana. "Let me hear it."

Layla gave a small smile of satisfaction. Her wish had been granted sooner than she had expected. Tariq and Jumana were going to confide in each other.

Tariq told his tale with the help of his new friends. Jumana listened, asking a question here and there for clarification. By the time Tariq finished, she was looking stunned.

"Rashid murdered? I can hardly believe it. I wanted answers, that's why I went outside the gate tonight. I thought I might finally learn why he wanted to delay the wedding. But murder? How is that possible?"

"Uncle Rashid wanted to delay the wedding?" asked Tariq.

"Yes, that was the argument we had in the courtyard."

"But…but…he didn't… we didn't…" Tariq spluttered.

Jumana repeated the story she had told Layla in the Garden of Dreams.

After she was done, Tariq said, "It must have been because of the anonymous letters."

"I wonder if we'll ever find out the truth," said Jumana. "It's been like a never-ending nightmare since Lamis's death."

"What was Lamis like?" asked Layla. "Did she seem out of whack in any way?"

"Not at all," said Jumana. "She seemed like a normal, intelligent woman. In retrospect, perhaps a bit too quiet and serious. The only person I saw her laughing with is the maid who came to clean our suites back then. They seemed very friendly."

"Lamis's suite was in this wing?" asked Layla.

"Yes, it was the last suite down this corridor," said Jumana. "Mrs. Haddad's suite is next to it."

"Does Mrs. Haddad know her suite is next to the dead tutor's?" said Zahra.

"We told her, and she didn't have a problem with it," said Tariq.

"Mrs. Haddad has nerves of steel," said Jumana. "She doesn't strike me as being the skittish sort."

"Who was the maid who cleaned your suites back then?" asked Zaid.

"It was Nura. She's a sweet girl but she seems so different now. Like she's afraid of her own shadow."

The teenagers shared a look.

Layla said, "If she was friends with Lamis, it gives her a good motive for being the Woman in White. It would also explain the incense sticks in the tower. But I don't know what she meant with that warning about evil to come."

"What incense sticks and what warning?" said Jumana.

They told her.

"It's all so mysterious," said Jumana when they were done. "I think we should speak to Nura and clear up these mysteries."

"I'll have her come to your suite after breakfast tomorrow," said Tariq.

"Yes, please do that." With a strange mixture of fear and anxiety in her amber eyes, Jumana said, "I have a feeling we're going to hear some momentous things tomorrow."

Chapter Twenty-One
Nura's Story

AFTER BREAKFAST THE next morning, they all gathered in Jumana's suite for the meeting with Nura. The maid arrived, wearing her customary allover black. She looked surprised to see them all there. Layla's heart leaped as she remembered Jumana's words from the night before. *I have a feeling we're going to hear some momentous things tomorrow.*

"Have a seat, Nura." Jumana gestured to a chair.

The maid sat down and folded her hands in her lap.

"Nura, we have some questions to ask you," said Tariq. "Is that okay with you?"

"Yes," she said, her cherubic face looking uneasy now.

"Were you friends with my tutor, Lamis?" asked Tariq.

Nura looked startled at the question. "Yes, we did get along well."

"Did she ever tell you anything about Rashid?" asked Jumana. There were dark circles under her eyes and a paleness to her face. From the way she gripped her hands, Layla could tell she was bracing herself for Nura's reply. *Poor Jumana. She must have lain awake last night, wondering what dark secrets would come to light about her dead fiancé.*

"No, Lamis never told me anything at all about Mr. Rashid," said Nura.

Jumana's relief was plain to see. "Did she tell you anything about herself?"

"She revealed that she was recovering from a divorce. From what she implied, I knew the marriage had been an unhappy one. She told me once she wouldn't ever marry again. She got her wish because she's dead now." There was a sheen of tears in the maid's eyes.

"I don't understand," said Jumana. "If Lamis didn't want to marry again, why did she steal my bracelet and kill herself?"

Nura's dark eyes flashed. "She wasn't the one who stole your bracelet. And she didn't kill herself either. Someone pushed her out that window." The maid's lips trembled, and tears filled her eyes.

The listeners looked at each other in shock.

"Why do you think that, Nura?" asked Jumana.

"On the evening your bracelet was stolen, I went up to Lamis' suite to refill her refrigerator. She was quiet and had a worried look on her face. I asked her what was wrong. She said, 'I think I know who stole Jumana's bracelet.' Shocked, I asked her who it was. She said, 'No, I can't tell you that. I could very well be wrong and accuse an innocent person.' When her body was found two mornings later, I knew she must have confronted the thief, who killed her and then framed her." Nura came to a stop, tears trickling from her eyes.

Jumana handed her a tissue.

"Nura, why didn't you tell this to the police when they came?" asked Tariq.

"I was afraid they wouldn't believe me," the maid whispered, wiping her tears. "I thought they would think I was making up the story and suspect me instead. Servants always get blamed when things are stolen. I couldn't afford to lose my job. My family depends on me. You can't imagine how wretched I've been since Lamis died. I felt like I've betrayed our friendship because I did nothing to clear her name. The one who killed her is still here. I can feel the evil. It's getting stronger and stronger. Sometimes I see Lamis in my dreams. I think she's trying to tell me something, but I don't know what. I feel like I'm going mad sometimes." The maid began to weep softly, her body rocking in a paroxysm of grief.

After Nura calmed down, Layla asked, "Are you pretending to be Lamis's ghoul, the Woman in White?"

"Of course not. I would never do such a thing. It would be an insult to Lamis."

"Do you know who might be doing it?" asked Zaid.

"No, I don't know who would do such a wicked thing. All the servants are puzzled and scared."

"We've seen you twice now by the lookout tower," said Adam. "Are you the one lighting the incense sticks there?"

"Incense sticks? No, I don't know anything about incense sticks. I go sometimes and look at the tower, wondering what happened that night. But I've never gone up there."

After a minute of silence, Tariq said, "Thank you for speaking with us, Nura. You can go now."

Looking relieved, the maid left the room, dabbing at her eyes.

"I don't know if Nura is telling the truth or if she's plain crazy," said Jumana. "If she's telling the truth, it means there's a murderer walking around scot-free. Oh, I wish Rashid had never given me that accursed bracelet."

Seeing their surprise, she said, "I don't really mean that. I know the bracelet wasn't to blame. But when a thing causes such ugliness, you can't help hating it."

"I think Lamis and Uncle Rashid's deaths are connected," said Tariq. "And *Al-Aqrab* is involved in it all."

"We should go see Aini tomorrow after *Jumu'ah*." said Zahra. "Maybe she's heard something new about *Al-Aqrab*."

"Alright, we'll go to a mosque in Khaldun and speak with Aini afterwards," said Tariq.

THE MOSQUE TARIQ took them to the next day, was a modern structure with spacious accommodations. The sermon was on the wisdom of the Creator in apportioning bounties and blessings in varying degrees to human beings. In all circumstances of life, there was a test involved, be one a pauper or a billionaire. The words resonated with Layla. Had she not seen evidence of this with her own eyes? Those who had much and those who had little were all tested alike, albeit in different ways.

When they went to look for Aini, the gypsy woman was not in her usual spot in front of the clothing store.

"She must have gone home or is running an errand," said Layla.

"Let's go ask in the clothing store," said Zahra. "Maybe they'll know where she is."

The owner of the clothing store was a heavyset man of middle years, dressed in a tan robe. He had shrewd eyes coupled with a smooth tongue. None of his customers left the store empty-handed. When they found him free for a moment, Tariq asked about Aini.

The storekeeper looked surprised. "You knew Aini?"

"Yes, we met her outside your store a couple of times," said Tariq. "We want to speak with her. Do you know if she went home?"

The man looked at them for a long moment. "Aini died three days ago."

The teenagers shared a shocked look.

"Oh, my God. How did it happen?" asked Layla.

"It was a hit and run accident. I don't know what the world is coming to these days. A poor woman gets killed and the driver takes off like nothing happened."

"Where did it happen?" asked Zahra.

"In her street as she was returning home that evening."

"Anyone saw what happened?" asked Adam.

"No, it was getting dark and the neighbors were all inside. One of them was coming home from work at about eight when he saw her body at the side of the road and called the police. Another reported that at about seven, she heard the impact of the car hitting Aini's body but didn't realize what it was at the time. When the ambulance and police arrived at about eight thirty, they said she had been dead for an hour. Maybe if someone had found her right away, they might have been able to save her. But Allah had decided her time was up and so Aini is gone. I'll miss her. She's been using my storefront for over two years."

"When was she buried?" asked Zaid.

"The day after she died. One of my customers whose nephew is a policeman, told me a strange thing."

"What was it?" asked Layla.

"Her nephew said Aini was clutching a dead scorpion when they found her. Odd, isn't it?"

The young people suddenly looked as if they had been turned to stone. The shopkeeper gave them a curious look, no doubt wondering at their strange reaction.

"Thank you for telling us," said Tariq at last.

They walked out of the clothing store and stood in the spot where Aini had sat. Hot tears filled Layla's eyes and she stifled a sob. *Poor Aini. The Scorpion must have murdered her because she spoke with us. She was right to be terrified of him. If we had left her alone, she wouldn't be dead now.* Layla had no idea how long they tarried in Aini's spot, giving in to the grief that had grabbed them by the throat.

Adam finally said, "Let's go to a café. We could all do with some tea right now."

Twenty minutes later, seated at a table in a secluded corner of a *Chat N Chai*, they sipped their beverages.

Zahra sniffled. "He killed her. It's our fault."

"Three days ago, was the day after she spoke to us," said Tariq. "He must have had spies watching us."

"We're probably being watched right now," said Zaid, his eyes darting about the cafe.

Layla balled her fists. "He must be stopped but we have no idea who he is."

"We know he's from a rich and powerful family and has a tattoo of a scorpion on his upper arm," said Zaid. "Maybe that information will come in useful."

"We have to find a way to expose him," said Adam. "Otherwise he's going to strike again. It might be close to home the next time."

THAT NIGHT, A persistent noise dragged Layla out of a deep sleep and brought her to wakefulness. She lay still for a few moments, wondering if it was the Woman in White. There were no sounds from her brother and friends, so it could not be the fake ghoul. She heard the noise again. It was a faint mewing and it seemed to be coming from the grove outside.

She glanced at the bedside clock. It was close to twelve. Sliding out from under the covers, she went over to the window and opened it. The mewing came from right below, a pitiful cry that tore at her heartstrings. It must be Bilqis. She must be hurt. There's only one thing to do. *I'll go see what's bothering her. I think I can handle it by myself without disturbing the others.*

Layla got dressed quickly, pulling on her black all-purpose

gown over her pajamas and grabbing a brown scarf. Through the open window, she could hear Bilqis's mewing escalating into angry yowls now. Hastily putting on her sneakers, she picked a comb and the flashlight she still had from their exploration of the dungeon. She hastened out of her suite and down the stairs.

At the bottom of the stairs, she wedged the comb in the door and entered the grove. Pale strips of moonlight spilled through the trees, casting swirling moonbeams on the ground below. Layla had never been unreasonably afraid of the dark. With a name that meant "night" she had always considered herself aptly named.

Turning on the flashlight, she followed the sounds of Bilqis's caterwauling to the huge *ghaf* beneath her window. When she looked down and saw two pinpoints of fire staring up at her, Layla almost screamed before she realized it was Bilqis's eyes. *How laughable it would have been if I had screamed and the others came down to the grove and caught me.* Pointing the flashlight down, she saw Bilqis had been trapped by a vine. It was wrapped around one of her paws and in her struggle to be free of it she had gotten even more entangled.

"Oh, you poor little kitty," Layla crooned. "Just stay still a minute and I'll get you away from the bad vine." She lowered the flashlight to the ground and began to untangle the vine.

Bilqis stared up at Layla, her eyes glittering like gems. When Layla freed her at last, the cat gave a soft purr of gratefulness and rubbed herself against Layla's legs.

"Twice now I've saved you," said Layla as she picked up the flashlight and stood up. "You owe me big time. What were you doing here anyway? Were you hunting a jerboa like the one you were chasing the other night? I'm afraid you'll have to take a rain check on that. Your paw is probably sore from that vine. Come, I'll take you inside."

The cat began hissing, her tail flailing from side to side. Layla froze as she heard the slight dragging of footsteps. Quickly, she turned off the flashlight, wondering if it was Hatem or the Woman in White. Moments later, she saw a white blur coming towards her. Her heart skipped a beat. *The Woman in White. I'll finally meet her face to face.*

The fake ghoul was garbed in her usual head to toe white with just the darkness of her eyes showing above the veil. As she drew closer, Bilqis vibrated with wrath. The cat backed up against Layla's legs with a ferocious hiss, causing Layla to lose her balance. As she flung out her hands to steady herself, the flashlight fell to the ground with a dull thud. Hearing the sound, the Woman in White came to a stop, her eyes probing the gloom. When she saw Layla, she spun on her heels and fled.

"Oh no, you don't," said Layla. "You're not getting away this time."

Thinking she might need the flashlight if the Woman in White went to hide in the orchard again, Layla scrabbled on the ground for it. She wasted precious moments but found it at last. She took off after the fake ghoul, vaguely aware of Bilqis at her heels.

The Woman in White had gotten a good head start. By the time Layla cleared the grove and raced into the inner courtyard, she saw a flash of white turning left towards the lookout tower. Layla sped across the courtyard and along the path towards the dark, towering structure. She arrived at the clearing just in time to catch a glimpse of white entering the tower. Still filled with the thrill of the chase, she continued to run until sudden realization hit her and she skidded to a dead stop.

The setting was eerily similar to the one in her dream. In it, she had stood at this same spot, staring up at the tower. In a quandary, Layla debated what to do next. *Should I go after the fake ghoul or should I play it safe and return to bed? If I returned to bed, I might never get this opportunity again.* A warm touch against her leg reminded Layla that Bilqis had kept pace with her. She bent and patted the cat.

"Let's go, Bilqis," she said, making up her mind. "I'm a little nervous but I can't miss this chance to catch the Woman in White. We need to solve this mystery once and for all. I mean, what could she do to me there? Push me down the stairs? I'm tall and strong. I'll make sure I hold on tightly to the rails. Come on, let's go"

As if she understood, Bilqis gave a soft purr, her large green eyes staring up trustingly at Layla.

Layla walked to the door of the tower and opened it. She winced when it gave a protesting squeak. The fake ghoul would have certainly heard it if she was just inside. Layla moved the flashlight around the entry and up the stairs. The Woman in White was not lurking there. She had gone up to the tower. Training the beam of the flashlight on the stairs, Layla began to climb, gripping the rails with her left hand. She kept a sharp lookout for the Woman in White. She did not want the fake ghoul to suddenly appear and startle her.

Bilqis padded behind her, and Layla could only marvel at the cat's intelligence. As she got closer to the top, her heart pounded in her ribs like a sledgehammer. When at last she reached the landing, the door stood closed and it was as silent as a grave. Had Layla not seen that fleeting flash of white, she would have thought she was the only human being here.

"I know you're in there, Woman in White," she called out. "Come out and show yourself. The game is up."

There was dead silence.

"You can't hide in there the whole night," said Layla. "I'd like to know why you're doing this."

Still dead silence.

I have to go in. She's not going to make this easy for me.

Taking a deep breath to ease the knot of fear in her stomach, Layla pushed open the door and almost ran back down the stairs. The empty rocking chair was moving slowly back and forth as if pushed by an unseen hand. Realizing that the Woman in White must have set it rocking when she fled behind the door, Layla went into the room. Before she could lose her nerve, she pulled the door forward, aiming the flashlight behind it. She cried out as she stared into dark eyes above a white veil.

The next moment, the veiled woman raised a small bullhorn and Layla felt a crushing blow on her right temple. Waves of pain radiated from the spot, blurring her vision and causing her to sag to the floor as darkness overcame her.

Chapter Twenty-Two
Horror in the Tower

L AYLA REGAINED CONSCIOUSNESS gradually, her eyes fluttering open as she became aware of her surroundings. A candle was flickering on the table. She was lying lopsidedly against a wall and had a painful crick in her neck. White strips of fabric were wrapped around her upper body, binding her arms to her torso. Her knees to ankles were similarly shackled, giving her the appearance of a half-shrouded mummy. The smell of incense came to her nostrils and memory returned in a flash. *The Woman in White. She hit me on the head.*

As her eyes darted around the room, a figure rose from the table, framed in the candlelight

"Mrs. Haddad," Layla gasped. "You're the Woman in White?"

"Ah, you've come to your senses," said the tutor as she held an incense stick to the candle flame. She sounded like a nurse speaking to a patient.

"Why have you tied me up?"

"You shouldn't have chased after me."

"Then you shouldn't go around pretending to be a ghoul."

"It was the only way I could have revenge on the Al-Khalilis."

"Revenge? Why do you want revenge on the Al-Khalilis?"

"They murdered my niece." Mrs. Haddad walked over to the fireplace, incense stick in hand. "They cold-bloodedly threw her out of this window."

"Lamis was your niece?"

"Yes, she was." Mrs. Haddad placed the smoking incense stick in the fireplace before seating herself in the rocking chair. "The family disowned her after she married that good-for-nothing against their wishes. After her marriage ended, she wrote that she was going abroad to become a tutor but didn't say where. I never heard back from her. I thought she wanted some space and time to recover, so I wasn't worried. It was a shock when we were informed of her death. The Al-Khalilis were generous with the blood money but I didn't believe the story they told her parents. Lamis never cared about jewelry. She would never have stolen a paltry bracelet. Nor would she have killed herself over a man."

"So, you came here to find out what you could?"

"Yes, it was easy for me to gain the position my poor niece had left vacant. The Al-Khalilis didn't know of my connection to her. I soon learned from a reliable source that they'd made up that story about her stealing the bracelet and committing suicide. They wanted to make her look like a scorned woman. But it was all a cover-up for what Rashid did to her."

"What did he do?"

"He molested her. When he became engaged to Jumana, Lamis threatened to tell her what he'd done. That sealed my poor niece's fate. Rashid and his father, that *cripple,*" Mrs. Haddad's lips curled with scorn, "coveted an alliance with Jumana's father, the powerful Governor of Tarub Province. They didn't want Lamis to thwart their plans. They hid the bracelet, faked a suicide letter and pushed her out that window."

Layla's brain was in a whirl. Her head had been hurting from

Mrs. Haddad's blow but now it throbbed even more. *Could it be true what Mrs. Haddad was saying? Had Lamis's death been a setup?* Reason quickly reasserted itself. Shaykh Sulaiman was an honorable man and would not have committed such a heinous act. From what she had heard of Rashid, he would not have done so either. Someone had fed Mrs. Haddad lies. It must be the same person who had stolen the bracelet and murdered Lamis.

"Mrs. Haddad, the Al-Khalilis didn't murder Lamis. She was murdered by the person who stole the bracelet. She told the maid, Nura, she knew who the thief might be. I bet it's the same person who told you all those lies."

"Rubbish. I have it on good authority the Al-Khalilis murdered her."

"Who told you that?"

"You don't need to know."

"So, you had Rashid murdered?"

"Of course not. He fell to his death in the desert."

"What about Tariq? Are you trying to kill him?"

"Why would I try to kill the boy when I'm here to give him lessons?"

"What about Jumana's kidnapping? Did you have anything to do with it?"

"When was Jumana kidnapped? That hit to your head must have affected your brain."

"So why are you pretending to be a fake ghoul? What kind of stupid revenge is that?"

Mrs. Haddad's eyes blazed. "I'll tell you why I'm doing this. It's because I'm hoping to come up with evidence against Rashid and his father. When Rashid met his just end, I only had his father left to destroy. I thought the stroke would be the end of the old man, but he still clings to life. The evidence is hard to come by. They told me to be patient, they'll find something for me soon. I've been biding my time pretending to be a ghoul, to remind the Al-Khalilis of their evil deed. Then they told me to come screaming in the grove at night. That it would embarrass the Al-Khalilis when you become scared and leave. They didn't bargain on you trying to catch me."

"Who are *they*?"

"*They* are of no concern to you."

"But why are *they* helping you against the Al-Khalilis?"

"It's none of your business."

"If you ask me, *they* are just using you."

Mrs. Haddad glared at Layla. "You're too meddlesome for your own good, do you know that? If you hadn't been so nosy, you wouldn't be here now."

Ignoring Mrs. Haddad's rant, Layla said, "*They're* only pretending to help you. *They'll* never be able to find any evidence against Shaykh Sulaiman because there's none."

"Be quiet. You talk too much."

"You're dealing with a dangerous villain. You think I don't know about the Scorpion?"

Mrs. Haddad gave Layla a suspicious look. "How do you know the scorpion is here? You were unconscious when I came back a few minutes ago."

"The Scorpion is here?"

"Yes, in a jar on the table."

"In…in a jar?" Layla croaked. Even as the horrific realization dawned on her, Mrs. Haddad went over to the table. She came back and stood over Layla, a small glass jar clutched in her hand. Inside, a black scorpion reared up, its tail thrashing against the side. Layla felt a rushing sound in her ears as her mouth went dry.

"This scorpion is for you," said Mrs. Haddad, as if she was presenting a gift to Layla. "They told me your death must look accidental. I don't have the heart to stay and watch. I'll place the jar on the ground and take the cover off before I leave. The scorpion will sense it's free and crawl out. Attracted by your body heat, it will sting you. I'm told that death is almost immediate."

Layla stared in horror at the scorpion in the jar. *Mrs. Haddad is mad. Stark raving mad.* "Please, Mrs. Haddad. Please don't do this."

"I must. I've come this far, I can't stop now. I must have the evidence I'm looking for to destroy Sulaiman ibn Al-Khalili. I cannot let you expose me. I'll leave the candle burning and will not gag you. No one will hear your screams anyway. The walls are too thick and the tower far away. I'll come back at dawn to remove your bonds. Hopefully, no one will realize you're missing before then. When you're found here, everyone will think you were stung by a scorpion when you came looking for the ghoul."

With those words, she stooped and set the jar in the middle of the floor. She removed the perforated lid and set it aside. Straightening up, she pivoted and went out the door, leaving Layla to contemplate the awful fate in store for her. Layla felt her skin prickle with revulsion as she looked at the thrashing scorpion. The creature must have sensed the barrier to its freedom had been removed. It began to crawl up the jar. Layla's heart pounded in time with the pounding of her temple where Mrs. Haddad had whacked her. As she watched with terrified eyes, the scorpion reached the opening. With a wiggle, it slithered out of the jar and on to the ground.

Chapter Twenty-Three
Layla's Long Night

As THE SCORPION swung its head towards her, Layla struggled against her bonds, but they remained unyielding. Had she been wearing her sneakers, she would have attempted to crush the creature with them. But Mrs. Haddad had removed them. The crafty woman must have anticipated that possibility. The missing footwear and the flashlight were sitting on the floor a few feet away. Layla watched in horror as the revolting creature began to crawl in her direction. It was like staring in the face of the snake charmer's cobra. *Déjà vu all over again.*

She knew screaming for help would not do any good. Even Bilqis had deserted her. Layla could not believe she was going to die alone in the tower, bitten by a scorpion of all things. She drew up her knees close to her trembling body. With her eyes fixed upon the approaching arachnid, she prayed for deliverance. The creature crawled relentlessly towards her. She tried shifting away, but it just altered its course to be in line with her body. There was no escape from it.

The scorpion was almost a foot and a half away when there came a pattering sound. Bilqis crept out from under the table.

The cat had not deserted her after all. She must have hidden from Mrs. Haddad. When Bilqis saw the scorpion, her hackles rose, and she gave a fearsome snarl. Her body crouched low, primed for attack.

"Don't touch it, Bilqis," said Layla. "It will sting you."

Seeming to understand, Bilqis made no move to get closer to the scorpion. Instead, she began to spit and snarl on the sidelines while the scorpion began to wave its tail madly in the air. As if conceding defeat, the loathsome creature began to crawl away in the direction of the fireplace. Further and further it went until it climbed up the wall of the fireplace and just hung there. Bilqis gave one last snarl as if to say, *you'd better not come down from there or else!*

"Good girl, Bilqis," Layla wept, thankful that she had been saved from the fatal sting of the deadly creature. Bilqis came and sat down next to her, the cat's warm body dispelling some of the chill that Layla had begun to feel. She felt comforted by the cat's presence. Should the scorpion crawl down the wall, Bilqis would chase it up again. Hopefully, she would not wander off down the stairs. *But what would happen when Mrs. Haddad returned and see me still alive? The crazed tutor might very well get the scorpion to finish me off then and there.*

Layla's temple throbbed as she thought of how she could outwit Mrs. Haddad. She would have to pray hard and use her wits to save herself. A vague plan began to form in her mind. Being the daughter of a doctor and a nurse, she had learned many interesting things at a young age. She was not certain her plan would work but she would have to give it a try.

It meant she would have to stay awake until Mrs. Haddad returned. In the meantime, she would get herself into position. She began to lower herself until she was laying full length on the floor. She tried to stay awake, but her mind began to lose focus and her eyes grew heavy with sleep. As exhaustion overwhelmed her, she soon succumbed to the beckoning sweetness of slumber.

LAYLA HEARD A sound and came awake. She stared at her surroundings in confusion. *Where in the world am I?* As she inhaled the familiar smell of incense, memory came rushing back. *Mrs. Haddad and the scorpion. Oh no, I must have fallen asleep.* She had no idea what time it was. The candle had burned out. All she could see was a pale patch of light coming from the top of the window.

Fearfully, she peered above the fireplace. The arachnid was still affixed to the wall. Layla sagged in relief. She saw that Bilqis napped faithfully by her side. Layla heard then what must have awakened her. The hollow slapping of footsteps coming up the stairs. Mrs. Haddad was returning. *Thank Allah I woke up in time to put my plan into action.* Bilqis opened her eyes and stood up. As if sensing danger, her mouth opened on a soundless snarl. She scurried under the table, blending with the dark shadows underneath. Layla was glad the cat had the good instinct to hide from Mrs. Haddad. Had the tutor seen Tariq's pet, she might have guessed what had happened.

As the footsteps drew closer, Layla let the saliva gather in her mouth. Making a face at having to do such an icky thing, she let it drip from the sides of her mouth. She began to groan as if in pain. Mrs. Haddad entered the room and stood rooted to the spot when she saw Layla still alive. From the corner of her half-closed eyes, Layla saw her looking around the room.

The tutor's gaze fastened upon the scorpion above the fireplace. "It must have bitten you before climbing up. I don't understand why you haven't died yet. I was told you would go quickly."

Seeing her ruse was working, Layla went into her final act. Tensing her body, she shook as if she was having convulsions. She gave a gurgle and ended with harsh, labored breathing. She kept this up as Mrs. Haddad hovered above her.

"I hate to see you suffer like this," Mrs. Haddad murmured. "I don't think it will be long now. You'll be gone before sunrise. And they told me I must go away for a few days." With those words, she pulled out a pair of scissors and began cutting away Layla's bonds.

Yes!

Mrs. Haddad gathered up the tattered bonds, took up the remains of the candle and hastened out the door. Layla waited until she could no longer hear the tutor's footsteps on the stairs. Sitting up, she began wiping the spittle off her face with her scarf. Her eyes went to the scorpion as it made a slight movement on the wall. There was one more icky thing she had to do. She forced her stiff limbs to move and got to her feet. Her head swam. She stood still for a few moments to let the dizziness pass. When she felt steady again, she bent down and picked up one of her sneakers. Walking over to the fireplace, she took a deep breath, steeling herself for what she was about to do. Lifting the sneaker, she brought it down on the scorpion.

She shuddered in revulsion at the squelching sound it made. Her stomach roiled but she kept on raining blows until the scorpion was just a gooey black pulp on the wall. There was no chance of it stinging anyone now. She wiped off the sneaker on the ground before sitting on the rocking chair and donning them both. Her temple ached, and she touched the swollen spot. *We were right. Mrs. Haddad had been using a bullhorn to make her banshee wail louder.*

Layla called out, "Bilqis, come girl. It's time we make our escape."

Bilqis came out from under the table, wrapped herself around Layla's feet and gave a heartfelt purr.

"I know. Me too," said Layla, reaching down to pat her. "I feel like a princess escaping from the wicked witch. Thank you for sticking with me. We're even now. Boy, won't the others be surprised to hear Mrs. Haddad was the Woman in White."

Bilqis hissed.

"You sensed the madness in her, didn't you?" asked Layla. "That's why you didn't like her."

WHEN LAYLA SET off for the castle, the white threads of dawn were giving way to a pale orange glow creeping up to the edge of the horizon. It would be sunrise soon and she was grateful she was still alive to see another day. She filled her lungs with the fresh morning air.

How precious life seemed after staring death in the face.

In the courtyard, Bilqis ran to one of the doors with a cat flap while Layla went through the arcade to the grove. A little knot of dread formed in the pit of her stomach. She was not looking forward to telling everyone her chilling tale.

By the time Jumana was summoned, Layla had showered and changed into a blue jersey dress and cream scarf. And the youths had ascertained that Mrs. Haddad had flown the coop. The deranged tutor had left a note saying she had to leave for a family emergency in Ghassan City. Her blue Range Rover was gone from the forecourt.

Adam had been furious with his sister for going after the Woman in White on her own.

"Were you out of your mind?" he had said. "First, it was the Mole Man with the cobra, now this. I wouldn't have been able to face Mom and Dad if that scorpion had bitten you."

"I'm sorry," Layla had said. "It seemed like a good idea at the time. I never thought she'd try to kill me."

Now, as Jumana was recovering from her shock at hearing the terrible tale, Tariq appeared with Dr. Hakam. In a stroke of good fortune, the doctor had been making one of his house calls to Shaykh Sulaiman. The youths had met him in the forecourt when they went looking for Mrs. Haddad's car. Tariq must have told the good doctor of what had happened and swore him to secrecy. After putting on gloves, he examined Layla's temple with gentle fingers, asking about her symptoms.

"Well, young lady," he said at last. "You've been very lucky. You don't seem to have a concussion. However, if you start to feel dizzy, nauseous, or your vision becomes blurred, go at once to the hospital in Khaldun. I'll leave you a few painkillers. Try not to do anything strenuous for the next couple of days."

Layla swallowed a tablet and fixed her scarf before joining the others in Zahra's suite. They were relieved Dr. Hakam had pronounced her fine. Tariq had been upset that a guest in the House of Al-Khalili should have undergone such an ordeal. The discussion now was on what to do about Mrs. Haddad.

"*Al-Aqrab* is probably protecting her right now," said Zaid. "The police won't find her."

"She didn't know who he was, anyway," said Adam. "We have to find the evil mastermind himself."

"We have to set a trap for him," said Zahra. "But I have no idea how we're going to do that."

Jumana, who had been in deep thought, said, "What if we set a trap by letting them kidnap me again?"

Chapter Twenty-Four
Setting a Trap

"OH, NO," SAID Tariq. "You can't use yourself as bait. It's too dangerous."

"I agree with Tariq," said Zaid. "It's too risky."

"We have to take the chance," said Jumana. "Allah knows who *Al-Aqrab* will murder next. We can't sit by and do nothing."

Tariq looked wretched. "How will you get them to kidnap you again?"

"At dinner this evening, we can talk about our plans for tomorrow. You can say what you plan to do and then ask me about my plans. I'll say that I'll be going for a ride to the foothills in the morning. I'm hoping it will reach the ears of *Al-Aqrab's* accomplices. If they still want to kidnap me, this will be their chance. Since they were planning to hide me in the caves for the first kidnapping, I'm assuming they'll want to do the same for the second one. Before I leave for my ride, you'll use the dungeon to go to the caves and lay in wait there. If the men do kidnap me and bring me there, you nab them. It should be easy for the group of you to tackle two men. We then call the police to make the men talk."

"What if they decide to take you somewhere else and not to the caves?" asked Zaid.

"They can't take me anywhere else on a horse in broad daylight. To be on the safe side, perhaps I should take a weapon with me."

"I'll give you a knife," said Tariq. "I wish we could keep in touch by cell phone, but they won't work underground or in the hills."

"Let's meet in my suite after breakfast so we can go over the plan," said Jumana.

Mindful of Dr. Hakam's advice, Layla spent the remainder of the day catching up on some much-needed sleep. Lunch was brought up to her room and by dinner she was feeling much better. Adam was concerned she was not well enough to join them in their undertaking the next morning. Layla would not hear of being left out. She felt she had earned the right to be there, come what may.

LAYLA HAD HEARD that Mrs. Haddad's hasty departure from the castle had been the hot topic at lunch. When they went down to dinner, Ghazala brought it up again.

"Mrs. Haddad should have told us what the emergency is," she said, her voice still scratchy from her bout of laryngitis. "Now we have no idea when she's coming back. It's very inconsiderate of her."

"Don't be hard on her, Ghazzy," said Suha. "She'll probably be back soon."

"I didn't even think she had family in Ghassan City," said Ghazala. "Did you know that when she applied for the position, Kareem?"

"No, she didn't mention that," said the PA.

Faisal grinned. "Maybe she wanted to have a few days off to have some fun. Teaching two hardheaded teenagers must have taken its toll on her."

"Hey, my head is not hard," said Hala. "I'll be glad when she's gone. She gave us too much homework. And she's weird and mean."

It takes one to know one.

"While she's away, I'll have more time to spend with our guests," said Tariq. "We plan to play some very interesting games tomorrow."

Hala looked bored. "Sounds tedious. My hairdresser from Khaldun is coming to put some highlights in my hair. That's way more interesting." Ever since the scene in the inner courtyard, she had been cold to them all.

"Do you want to join us for some games tomorrow, Jum-Jum?" asked Tariq.

"No, I'll leave you teenagers to it. I'm planning to go for a ride to the foothills in the morning. I need to get some exercise. All this wonderful food has made me put on some extra pounds. After I come back, I'll have a nice, long swim."

Layla covertly watched the faces around the table for a reaction. But there were no facial expressions out of the ordinary. Not even a slight start or a shifty-eyed look. *If any of Al-Aqrab's accomplices are here, they could probably win Oscars for their acting ability.*

"I'm going to Khaldun in the morning," said Faisal. "Don't say I didn't tell you."

I wonder why he goes to Khaldun so much. Maybe he's been meeting Al-Aqrab?

"I'm going there in the morning too," said Kareem. "I'll probably return after lunch."

Layla glanced sideways at the PA. *He seems like family the way he blends in. He's perfect for the part of Al-Aqrab's accomplice.*

Ghazala said, "We're going to Khaldun too. Bilal needs some supplies."

Hmm, rather sudden.

Bilal nodded in wordless agreement. *What an odd man he is. He hardly speaks for himself and seems to be buried in his books most of the time. Is he a genuine scholar or is that a front for something more sinister?*

Miftah struggled to cover a burp but lost the battle when his body betrayed him. The hiccupy sound filled the air and had the same effect as a car backfiring. Everyone winced.

"I guess Suha and I are the only ones who don't have any plans for the morning," he said. Patting his ample stomach, he added, "I should probably get some exercise myself."

Layla looked at Suha, whose face wore a stoic expression. *It has to be hard for her, married to an older man who has some rough edges. On top of that, she has a stepdaughter who hates her.*

The meal ended with no sign that any of *Al-Aqrab's* accomplices were at the table and were going to take the bait.

AFTER BREAKFAST THE next morning, the teenagers sprang into action. They changed into more appropriate apparel and concealed their flashlights as they headed to the dungeon. Layla had been told the plan was to leave the dungeon at ten and be at the entrance of the caves by eleven-fifteen. For her part, Jumana would be leaving Dukhan Castle at eleven, arriving at the foothills by eleven-thirty. This would give the teenagers a fifteen-minutes head start before they expected to see any activity.

In the dungeon, Tariq brought the pouch he had carried in the Nawaf Desert and a giant canvas bag. From the pouch, he pulled out the two hunting knives, giving one to Adam and keeping the other for himself.

"I don't know if the kidnappers will have any weapons," he said. "If they do, I hope we'll be able to catch them by surprise before they use them on us."

From the canvas bag, he took out two coils of sturdy rope. "I'll carry one and you can carry the other," he said to Zaid. "It's always good to take ropes to the caves. We can use it to tie up the kidnappers if we catch them. Let's wrap it around our waists."

After the youths completed that task, Tariq pulled out his cell phone and said, "Alright, it's ten on the dot. Let's move."

With Tariq in the vanguard, followed by Zaid, Zahra, Layla and Adam, they set off from the dungeon. The flashlights lit up the thick darkness around them. They soon came to the point where the rock tunnel ended and the rough-hewn one began. When they reached the end of the tunnel, they moved stealthily in order not to rouse the bats again. The secret aperture remained open from their last visit and one by one they passed through into the cave beyond.

As Layla was about to enter, she heard a slight shuffling sound and wondered if they had disturbed the bats again. She slid quickly through the opening, Adam following right behind.

Tariq said, "Remember those pits and shafts. Let's go."

They had not gone very far when they heard an echoing cry of distress.

"Help!"

"What in the world was that?" asked Adam.

"It sounds like someone in trouble," said Zaid.

"The sound came from behind us," said Layla.

"It must be a spelunker," said Tariq. "Some of them come on their own to explore. He must have fallen down a pit and hurt himself. We'll have to go help him."

"But what about Jumana?" asked Zahra.

"Help!" The cry came again, louder this time and more insistent.

The teenagers came to a stop, in an agony of indecision on what to do next.

Zahra was the one who suggested a solution for their dilemma. "Why don't we split up in two groups? One group go ahead and act as lookouts while the other helps the spelunker."

"I suppose we'll have to do that," said Tariq.

"I remember how to get to the large cave," said Zaid. "Zahra and I can go act as lookouts. The three of you can look for the spelunker."

"Here, you take the knife." Adam handed Zaid the weapon.

Tariq pulled out his cell phone and looked at the time. "We have half an hour before Jumana gets to the foothills. Here's what we'll do. My group will look for the spelunker and see if we can help him. If he's not hurt, we'll ask him to come with us. We'll go hide in the great cave. Zaid, you and Zahra will go to the entrance and keep watch for Jumana and the men. If you see them, keep out of sight and see where they hide her. Don't show yourselves unless she's in immediate danger. Once you know where she is, you come meet us in the great cave. We'll all go tackle the kidnappers together."

"What if the spelunker is hurt?" asked Zahra.

"We'll have to get help for him after we tackle the kidnappers," said Tariq.

"What if the kidnappers leave?" asked Zaid.

"That's going to mess up our plan," said Adam.

"They'll have to bring food and water to Jumana," said Layla. "I don't think they plan to starve her. We'll be able to catch them at some point in time."

"Yes, that's true," said Tariq. "Zaid and Zahra, you get going and we'll do the same."

Zaid and Zahra were quickly swallowed up in the bowels of the cave while Tariq, Adam and Layla turned around and began to follow the echoes of distress.

"We're coming to help you," Tariq cried. "Keep calling."

The echoes from his voice faded away and were replaced by the echoes of distress, which sounded very close.

"The sound seems to be coming from the same direction we came from," said Adam. "That's weird. We didn't see any spelunker there."

"He must have been coming from another cave," said Tariq. "Remember, they're all connected like a honeycomb."

They continued forward, Tariq keeping his flashlight trained on the ground ahead.

Then they saw it. A gaping hole in their path where the earth had caved in.

The cry of distress came once more.

Layla said, "It sounds like a child."

There was silence. Then a plaintive voice said, "It's me. Hala."

Chapter Twenty-Five
In the Caves

"HALA," THEY EXCLAIMED, their voices blending together to produce a jumble of echoes.

Tariq moved cautiously to the edge of the pit and shined his flashlight down it. "Hala, how did you get here?"

"I was following you." Hala's voice sounded tearful. "Then I fell into this hole."

It was her I must have heard making that shuffling sound.

"Are you hurt?" asked Adam."

"No, I just want to get out of here."

"Don't worry, we'll get you out," said Tariq. "You're too far down for us to pull you out. We're going to throw a rope. Tie it around your waist so it doesn't squeeze you. Grab onto it and we'll lift you out."

"We can tie the other end of the rope to that rock over there." Layla pointed to a narrow slab of rock protruding from the cave wall. "That way, we won't lose hold of it."

"Yes, we can wind it around the rock to help bear Hala's weight," said Adam.

"That's an excellent idea," said Tariq. After unwinding the

coil from around his waist, he handed one end to Adam to fasten to the slab of rock. He lowered the other end into the pit. "Grab the rope, Hala."

"I can't," Hala wailed. "What if you drop me?"

Layla moved forward and aimed her flashlight into the pit. She could see Hala huddled about eight feet below, looking terrified. Even though the other girl had been mean to her, she felt nothing but pity right now.

Sounding exasperated, Tariq said, "Hala, you'll have to grab on to the rope and tie it around your waist. It's the only way we can get you out."

Hala began to sob. "I want my *Abu*. Send for him."

"There's no time for that," said Adam. "We can get you out."

"No, you can't," said Hala. "Why did you have to come to this stupid place, anyway?"

Layla quickly went from feeling pity to irritation. "Listen, Hala," she snapped. "Jumana is going to be kidnapped and we need to be there. You're wasting our precious time behaving like a baby. Take hold of the rope and tie it around your waist. Otherwise, we'll darn well leave you here."

"Jumana kidnapped?" Hala sounded shocked. "What's going on?"

"We don't have time to explain," said Adam. "Now, are you going to grab the rope or not?"

"I'll grab it." Hala's voice was chastened.

Tariq took up his position close to the lip of the pit, followed by Layla and Adam. Layla hoped they would not all end up in the pit with Hala. With a deep breath, Tariq braced himself and pulled on the rope. Layla gritted her teeth and grabbed it with all her strength. Adam strained to wrap the rope coming up from the pit around the rock. Layla breathed a little easier as the edges of the pit held fast and did not crumble under their weight.

They grunted with the strain of hauling Hala up. Layla's

palms were burning, and her arms were aching. She knew they would have painful blisters from gripping the rope. Hala would not get off easy either. She would have multiple bruises by the time they pulled her out.

Layla chafed at the delay as the minutes flew by. The pit was deep, and they were making slow progress. Jumana must be on her way to the foothills by now. Would the kidnappers show up? If they did, would they bring Jumana to the caves? They can't take her away on a horse in daylight but what if they transferred her to a waiting car? *We didn't think of that possibility.* Layla's heart sank. A cunning foe such as *Al-Aqrab* would realize that carrying Jumana off in the confines of a car would make better sense than carrying her off on horseback. *If only we could be on our way to see what's happening.*

To Layla's relief, they began to make progress. Hala's head appeared at the edge of the pit and with one final pull, she was resting halfway over the lip. Tariq reached down and grabbing her by the shoulders, pulled her to safety. They all stood for a minute, recovering their strength and rubbing their hands where the rope had abraded their skin.

"Thank you," Hala said in a small voice.

"Why did you do such a stupid thing and follow us?" Tariq finally gave vent to his anger. "You were lucky we heard you and that pit wasn't a sinkhole."

"My hairdresser canceled our appointment." Hala's voice was sullen. "Since I had nothing to do, I thought I would come see what games you were playing. You weren't in the recreation area but one of the maids said she'd seen you go to the door of the dungeon. I was curious, so I got a flashlight and followed you. I didn't really care for these dark caves, so I turned back to return. That's when I fell into the hole."

She probably canceled the appointment with the hairdresser, so she could keep tabs on Tariq.

"I suppose you'll have to stay with us now," said Tariq, as he began to untie the rope from around Hala's waist.

The knot, which had borne the girl's weight, proved stubborn. Layla took Tariq's hunting knife and lopped it off. Adam unwind the rope from around the rock. After Tariq wrapped it around his waist again, they set off for the great cave. Layla was sure Jumana would have been kidnapped by now if *Al-Aqrab* had given the order. She did not voice her earlier fears to the youths. They would learn the outcome soon enough. Her temple throbbed from all the thinking she was doing. Still not fully recovered from her escapade the night before, she felt tired and sluggish as they trudged through the dark maw of the caves. They reached the great cave and saw a dim light radiating from it.

"Everyone, freeze," a harsh voice called out.

The teenagers stared in shock as two men stepped out of the darkness and shone flashlights in their faces.

"It's more of those kids," the first man said. Layla drew in a sharp breath when she saw who the second man was. It was the Mole Man. Each of the men were holding a long rifle.

"Search them," the Mole Man said to his companion.

With the Mole Man's rifle trained on them, they had no choice but to submit to the search. Tariq's dagger was seized though they left the rope around his waist.

"*Ta'al.* Come," the Mole Man growled.

He and his cohort shoved the teenagers across the cave. In the light of the flashlights, they saw Jumana, Zaid and Zahra huddled under a huge formation of stalactites, their hands and feet bound. They all exchanged silent looks of dismay. The Mole Man's partner unwound the rope from around Tariq's waist. He used the confiscated hunting knife to cut the rope into portions. He tied the new prisoners one by one while the Mole Man kept his rifle pointed at them. Hala struggled for a moment, but the man grabbed her roughly. Looking miserable and frightened, she did not resist again.

"What do you mean to do with us?" asked Tariq after they had been bound and dumped on the ground with the other prisoners.

"That's for *Al-Aqrab* to decide," said the Mole Man.

"You cowardly crook," said Layla. "You won't get away with this, just wait and see."

To Layla's fury, the two men laughed. She was about to let loose another blistering set down when a third man appeared at the head of the cave, speaking excitedly in Domari. The Mole Man and his partner sprinted out of the cave with the third man, taking their own flashlights and leaving the seized ones to provide light. The prisoners all began to speak at once.

Tariq said, "One at a time, please. Tell us what happened, Jumana."

Jumana said, "The kidnappers were ready and waiting when I set off on my ride. Within five minutes, they grabbed me and brought me here at breakneck speed. I guess they weren't taking any chances of me being rescued again. When we came, two men were already here."

"Yes, they were waiting here for the other two men to bring Jumana in," said Zaid in a disgusted voice. "Zahra and I walked right into them. Five of us might have stood a chance against them but two of us didn't. Not when they carried rifles. They tied us up with the rope I had around my waist."

Layla glared at Hala. It was her fault they had all been caught and tied up with their own ropes.

"There was no way we could have warned you," said Zahra. "The Mole Man and his friend have been guarding us since they caught us. I think the other two are keeping watch at the cave entrance. They're probably waiting to hear from *Al-Aqrab.*"

"Something must have happened, that's why the third man

came to get these two," said Adam. "Maybe they've heard from *Al-Aqrab.*"

"What a fiasco this has turned into," said Jumana. "We miscalculated and now we're at the mercy of *Al-Aqrab.*"

They were all silent for a moment as they contemplated their predicament.

"How come Hala's with you?" asked Jumana.

Tariq explained what had happened. Hala's expression was downcast, as if she knew her sneaky stunt would not endear her to him in the least. They became quiet as they heard voices and saw three people being shoved into the cave by the Mole Man and his companion.

It was Hatem, Miftah and Suha.

"Abu," Hala cried in surprise.

Miftah's eyes probed the dimness of the cave and he looked dumbfounded to see them all.

"How did you all get here?" he exclaimed. Turning to their captors, he said, "I don't know what the meaning of this is, but you'd better release us if you know what's good for you."

Ignoring him, the Mole Man and his partner started to tie the threesome with the leftover rope. Miftah glared at them while Suha looked angry and agitated. In contrast, the head groom stood silent and impassive. After the three new prisoners had been restrained and set on the ground, the Mole Man and his partner settled down to wait again. They looked up as their other two companions burst into the cave, gesticulating and speaking agitatedly in Domari. After a minute of frenzied back and forth, all four men left, still speaking heatedly.

"Abu, how did you know we were here?" asked Hala.

"We didn't," said Miftah. "We came to rescue Jumana."

"You came to rescue me?" said Jumana. "How did you know I needed rescuing?"

"I told him," said Hatem. "When you went riding alone, I was worried. Especially after you were kid…it's not always safe for a woman to ride alone. I asked Raj to follow you. He soon came back in a panic, saying you had been grabbed by two men who were riding towards the hills."

Layla's eyes narrowed as she stared at Hatem. *I'm sure he had been about to say kidnapped. How had he known Jumana had been kidnapped before? He seemed to be an ally, so he couldn't be Al-Aqrab's accomplice. Was he the Hooded Horseman?*

Miftah said, "Since all the others had gone to Khaldun, Hatem told me and Suha. We called the police but didn't know how long it would take them to get here. They're a slow lot in Khaldun. Hatem said he was coming to look for you and Suha and I decided to come with him. When we got to the hills, two men pulled guns on us and forced us to come here. Now tell us how you all got here."

They looked at one another. Who would start the tale and where would they start from?

At that moment, they heard a great clamor, waves of sounds that vibrated around the cave like distant thunder. To Layla, it sounded like a herd of wild elephants all trumpeting at once. They looked at each other in mystification. What could be causing the commotion?

The sounds became fainter until there was silence once more.

"I wonder what that was all about," said Zaid.

"It sounded like the Mole Man and his partners were having a really loud shouting match," said Adam.

A shadow moved at the head of the cave. As they stared at the spot, a man stepped forward into the circle of light. He was wearing a hood with a covering that concealed almost his whole face. In his hand, he held a rifle and a dagger.

"The Hooded Horseman," Adam exclaimed.

"Who are you?" demanded Miftah.

"A friend," came a low, deep voice.

"Then show us who you are," said Jumana.

Without a word, the Hooded Horseman pulled the hood from his head and the covering off his face. There were exclamations of shock.

"Uncle Rashid!" Tariq cried.

Chapter Twenty-Six
Shocking Surprises

"**N**O, IT CANNOT be you." Suha looked at Rashid, her eyes wild. "*Al-Aqrab* told me you're dead. How can you still be alive?"

There was a shocked silence.

Layla cried, "Suha is *Al-Aqrab's* accomplice."

"Who's *Al-Aqrab?*" said Miftah.

"He's a monster who's got blood on his hands," said Hatem, to their surprise.

"Suha," Miftah said in a dreadful voice. "Is this true?"

"Yes, it's true," Suha spat out. She rose to her feet, throwing aside the ropes *Al-Aqrab's* men must have just wrapped around her. Gone was the amicable woman they knew. In her place stood a shrew, her eyes looking wild in the glow from the flashlights.

"Who's *Al-Aqrab?*" asked Rashid. "And what does he want?"

Suha gave a brittle laugh. "He's your own blood. And he'll get what he wants when you're all dead. His men will soon return and put bullets in you. Or maybe *Al-Aqrab* will send some of his scorpions to sting you to death."

Layla shuddered. She was relieved when Rashid said, "Your

men won't do any good unless they learn to fly. I lured all four of them into a deep shaft. You must have heard them shouting and cursing at me."

So that's the commotion we heard.

"There are always more men…and women." Suha pulled a revolver from her pocket and held the weapon to Hala's head. "Throw down your rifle and knife," she told Rashid. "Or I'll shoot Hala in the head."

Her voice rose an octave higher as she screamed, "Do it now!"

With reluctance, Rashid threw down his weapons and Suha moved forward and kicked them into the darkness. With the pistol now trained on Rashid, she said, "Untie Hala's hands and feet."

Rashid complied and a minute later, Hala was free. Suha then ordered Hala, "Take the rope and tie Rashid's hands behind his back. Tie it tightly and don't do anything stupid or you'll get a bullet in you."

With a glare at her stepmother, Hala began to tie Rashid's hands.

"Tie it tighter," Suha said in a shrill voice.

After Rashid's hands were tied, Suha commanded, "Now both of you go and sit with the others."

"You wicked witch," said Hala. "I knew your sweetness was all a pretense. You're rotten to the core."

"Shut up." Suha's face was a mask of hate as she raised her hand and gave Hala a violent slap across the face. Hala screamed as she stumbled with the force of the blow. She cowered before her stepmother. *How the tables have turned.*

"You had that coming, you spoiled brat," said Suha. "I've wanted to do that for a long time."

"How could you do this, Suha?" asked Miftah. He seemed to have aged ten years in ten minutes. "How could you do this to us?"

"He's the one to blame." She pointed an accusing finger at Rashid. "He should have married me. But I had to settle for a disgusting old man like you."

Miftah drew back as if she had slapped him. He stared at her in dazed silence.

"You were the one sending those anonymous letters, weren't you?" Rashid said to Suha.

"Yes, it was me," said Suha in a gloating voice.

"What were the letters about?" asked Jumana.

Suha chuckled. "They warned your beloved fiancé not to marry you or he'd die a horrible death. I signed them with Lamis's name. I could see how they rattled him."

Jumana looked at Rashid in shocked comprehension. "So that's why you were acting strange and wanted to delay the wedding. Why didn't you tell me, instead of letting me think the worst?"

"I didn't want to worry you," said Rashid. "I was also embarrassed because I suspected someone from the household was sending them. I thought you might have second thoughts about marrying me if you found out. The last letter came while you were there. It was so poisonous, I got alarmed. I thought it best to delay the wedding until I found out who was responsible. I'm sorry for all the distress I caused you. Please forgive me."

"How touching," Suha sneered. "Do you know why he was alarmed about that last letter, Jumana? It's because I accused him of molesting Lamis and other maids at the castle. And I threatened to tell you and your father if Rashid didn't call off the wedding. Imagine how your dear father would have felt had he gotten such a letter. He would have called off the wedding at once. I'm sure he wouldn't have wanted such a molester for a son-in-law."

"You're despicable, Suha." Jumana's voice trembled. "How could you tell such filthy lies?"

"You think I was going to let him marry you when he had rejected me?"

"Is that why *Al-Aqrab* tried to kill me?" asked Rashid. "So I wouldn't marry Jumana?"

"No, the plan was to prevent the wedding, not kill you. But on the night of your argument with Jumana, I saw you going to Tariq's suite. I wanted to know if you would tell him what you and Jumana had argued about. I hid in the sitting room while you were in the bedchamber. I heard you telling him you were receiving anonymous letters. That you were planning to go to Ghassan City and find a private investigator to come and investigate. We couldn't allow that to happen, so *Al-Aqrab* decided to get rid of you. We weren't worried about Tariq because he was sick at the time and seemed to have fallen asleep. But one of our men heard him talking to the guests in the garden. Tariq told them he suspected you were murdered though he couldn't recall much of what you told him. We couldn't take the chance of him remembering. *Al-Aqrab* decided Tariq had to be eliminated too."

"I guess that explains the stone in Jasim's saddle and the scorpion on my bed," said Tariq.

"When did you decide to bring the investigator to the castle?" Jumana asked Rashid.

"After our meeting in the courtyard," said Rashid, sharing a look with her that spoke volumes.

"What about us?" asked Zaid. "Why was the Mole Man following us in Ghassan City? Was he the one who pushed Zahra in front of that car?"

"The Mole Man?" Suha looked puzzled. Then she giggled. "Oh, you mean Wajdi. Yes, *Al-Aqrab* told him to make sure something happened to one of you but Wajdi bungled it."

"But why did *Al-Aqrab* want to harm us?" said Zahra

"He wanted you to leave. He had a grand scheme up his sleeve and didn't want visitors here when he carried it out. That's why we told the Woman in White to scare you. And why we locked you in the dungeon. But it didn't work. The same goes for Jumana. We wanted to scare her away, that's why *Al-Aqrab* arranged her first kidnapping. But Wajdi's men were incompetent. When we found out the gypsy woman had been running her mouth off, *Al-Aqrab* took care of her. Then Layla found out Mrs. Haddad was the ghoul. I gave Mrs. Haddad the scorpion to take care of Layla but Mrs. Haddad botched it. *Al-Aqrab* was furious because that was the end of his grand scheme, thanks to these wretched kids."

"Why kidnap me today then?" asked Jumana.

Suha chuckled. "It was for the ransom your dear Papa would have paid to get his precious little girl back. We had no idea you were going to set a trap. Now *Al-Aqrab* will have to get us out of this mess. I called him before we left. Miftah thought I was calling the police." She threw a scornful look at her husband.

"What was *Al-Aqrab's* grand scheme?" asked Tariq.

"I can't give away all our secrets now, can I? But I'll give you a hint. Mrs. Haddad would have played the leading role."

"If you tell us who *Al-Aqrab* is, we'll let you go and start a new life elsewhere, Suha," said Rashid. "You don't have to listen to him anymore."

"I don't want to go anywhere else," Suha shrieked, stamping her foot like a child who was being denied a toy. "Before my father died, he told me to stay at the castle and make sure you marry me. He said it was my right and I was entitled to it. If you hadn't refused to marry me, none of this would have happened."

As Layla listened to Suha, other pieces of the puzzle fell into place. "You're the one who stole Jumana's bracelet and pushed Lamis out of the tower, didn't you, Suha? When you found out Mrs. Haddad was Lamis's aunt, you fed her a bunch of lies so she would fall in with your plans."

"You've figured it out, have you?" Suha shoved the gun in her pocket and sat down on a rock several feet away. "It was

Lamis's own fault that she died. My favorite diamond pin fell off outside Jumana's suite when I took the bracelet. Lamis found it when she passed by and put two and two together. She had the nerve to tell me I should return the bracelet, or she would tell the family I stole it. I told her not to tell anyone, and to meet me in the tower at midnight so we would talk more about it. She was gullible enough to fall for it. One of *Al-Aqrab's* men was lying in wait behind the door and helped throw her out the window."

"How did you get Mrs. Haddad to believe your lies?" asked Zahra.

"It was after Rashid had supposedly died. I caught her going through the drawers in the office late one night. I had gone to see if I'd left my cell phone there. She told me a lame lie about looking for a map. I suspected she was up to something. I searched her room the next day and found an old letter from Lamis. That's how I learned who she was. When I confronted her, she told me she was trying to find out the truth of Lamis's death. That she suspected foul play, that's why she became the Woman in White. She pleaded with me not to tell anyone. I told *Al-Aqrab* and that's how he came up with his grand scheme. To make sure Mrs. Haddad helped us, I told her that Rashid and Sulaiman were to blame for Lamis's death. That I myself was molested by Rashid. And someone who was also wronged by the family would help us to find the evidence she needs. Mrs. Haddad was getting impatient. That's why she took matters in her own hands and screamed in Sulaiman's room that night. When I came back from Ghassan City, I convinced her we were close to finding some evidence. That she would get it before she leaves. She believed every word I told her. She and Lamis were stupid women for all their education."

There came a shriek from the head of the cave.

"Suha!"

Mrs. Haddad erupted into the cave, dressed in a long black gown and holding a flashlight in her hand.

"You lied to me," she screamed at Suha. "You killed Lamis."

Suha got to her feet. "Mariam, how did you get here?"

Mrs. Haddad looked at Suha with burning eyes. "After you sent me to hide in Khaldun, I started to think about what Layla told me that night. I became guilt-stricken and began to have doubts about you. I had to speak to Nura to know if Layla was telling the truth. I took a taxi back to the castle, wearing a face veil like some of the maids so I wouldn't be recognized. I found Nura and she told me what I wanted to know. She said Layla was alive. But you didn't have the decency to tell me, did you?"

"You botched it," Suha said with a contemptuous curl of her lips. "You should have stayed in Khaldun."

"That would have suited you, wouldn't it?" said Mrs. Haddad. "My mistake was in telling you what Layla told me. I realize now you wanted me out of the way, so I wouldn't question Nura. I was going in search of you when Nura told me you and your husband had left to go rescue Jumana in the caves. I became suspicious. I got a horse from the stables and came here. While I was hiding to see what was going on, I saw a hooded man coming. I followed him into the caves but lost him along the way. It took me a while to find you, but I did, and I heard everything you said. You almost made me commit murder because of your lies. You were using me all this time. You made me apologize to Ghazala after our argument, so the Shaykh wouldn't fire me. You wanted to keep me here for your own evil ends. I won't let you get away with this…," Mrs. Haddad's voice trailed away as she advanced towards Suha, an implacable look on her face.

"Mariam, stay back," said Suha. "I have a gun in my pocket and I won't hesitate to use it."

"I have nothing more to lose now," said Mrs. Haddad. "I'm already a criminal because I believed your lies."

With sudden swiftness, she pulled a short knife from her pocket and lunged at Suha. Suha dodged the knife and latched on to Mrs. Haddad's hand. With a strength that belied her slender frame, Mrs. Haddad jerked her hand free. Before she could raise the knife, Suha grabbed hold of the tutor's hand again. The two women struggled together, grunting and snarling like wild animals determined to draw blood. Across the cave they grappled with each other, watched by the helpless prisoners.

Suha stumbled over a dip in the ground, losing her grip on Mrs. Haddad's hand. With a guttural cry, the tutor's lips drew back in a snarl. She raised the knife and plunged it into Suha's stomach. Suha gave a piercing scream and swayed like a tree in the wind. Panting, she fumbled for the gun and pulled it out of her pocket. She aimed it at Mrs. Haddad with shaking hands and fired. The weapon went off with a thunderous bang, hurting the eardrums of the prisoners and fouling the air with an acrid stench.

The cave trembled with a frenzy of echoes, loosening bits and pieces of rock which rained down upon the prisoners like hailstones. Layla shielded her face as best as she could, hoping the stalactites would not break off and come toppling down on them. Thankfully, the tapering icicles withstood the tremors and remained in place.

The prisoners watched as Mrs. Haddad staggered and fell against Suha, the knife dropping out of her hand. The two women swayed together in a grotesque embrace. All of a sudden, the earth seemed to swallow them up. They vanished from sight, their cries echoing in the cave until there was abrupt silence.

Chapter Twenty-Seven
An Amazing Tale

RASHID CALLED, "HALA, look for my knife. We've got to cut these ropes and rescue them."

Hala located the knife and one by one, as the prisoners were freed, they went over to the gaping hole where the two women had fallen in. A sense of unreality took hold of Layla as they shined flashlights into the deep pit and called out to the women. But it was to no avail. Suha and Mrs. Haddad were beyond the range of sight and sound. In the end, it was determined they must be unconscious or dead. Or they must have fallen down a sinkhole that ran deep underground. The task of searching for them would have to be left to the professionals.

The sun was past its zenith by the time the prisoners returned to the castle. Layla was glad their horses had been brought for them to ride back. She had not been looking forward to a long walk through the dungeon again. Dhul Fikar must have been on the lookout for them. He was waiting at the door when they entered the castle from the inner courtyard. When he caught sight of Rashid, he blinked and did a good impression of a fish gasping for water on land. The others had all returned from

Khaldun and it was almost comical to see their reactions when they saw Rashid.

"Rashid," Ghazala gasped, her hand going to her heart. "How…how…" words seemed to fail her.

"All our tears were in vain it seems, my dear cousin," said Faisal, as blasé as ever.

"You must have quite a tale to tell us," said Kareem.

"I thought this only happened in books and movies," said Bilal.

When Ghazala began peppering him with questions, Rashid raised his hand and said, "You'll learn everything this evening, I promise. Right now, I need to clean up and go see Father."

"Where's Suha?" Ghazala looked around. "I thought she went with you, Miftah."

There was an awkward silence.

Miftah said in a wooden voice, "There was an accident. Suha and Mrs. Haddad fell into a sinkhole. We've sent for a team of spelunkers to search for their bodies."

"They're dead?" Ghazala swayed with shock. "But wasn't Mrs. Haddad in Ghassan City? How did she get to the caves?"

"They'll tell us later," said Bilal, placing an arm around his wife's shoulder. "Let them recover first."

THE TEENAGERS ATE late lunches in their rooms and settled down for a rest. Before dinner, Tariq came by to tell them his grandfather and Uncle Rashid had a most emotional reunion. Shaykh Sulaiman had been overjoyed his son was alive. Father and son had clung to each other as they shed tears together. Rashid had then given his father and Tariq a condensed version of the events that had occurred on that fateful day.

"I won't tell you anything," said Tariq. "You have to hear it from Uncle Rashid himself. It's unbelievable."

Tariq's little snippet had only served to keep the teenagers in a state of suspense during the rest of the evening. Finally, it was time for explanations and they all headed to the domed hall. All the family was there, as well as Kareem, Hatem and Nura. Shaykh Sulaiman was brought in by Qais on his wheelchair, looking happy and so much healthier than before. As everyone settled in their seats in the domed hall, an expectant hush fell over the assembly.

Rashid began his tale, filling in the blanks they had not yet heard. He had made his usual tour of the desert and then headed to Gurian Plateau to look for the lizards. When he reached the valley, it was time for the midday prayer. He went to the lake, took off his watch and began to make ablution. Hearing a sound behind him, he spun around to see two masked men almost upon him. He had no time to defend himself for the next moment, one of them hit him on the back of his head and the world went black around him. When he was in possession of his senses again, he found himself caught in the spreading branches of a tree growing out of a crevice on the overhang of the plateau.

Rashid said, "I realized that the men who had ambushed me must have thrown me over the plateau, hoping I would be smashed to death on the rocks below. Miraculously, the tree had broken my fall and cushioned me from serious injury. I was bleeding from the blow to my head and a deep gash on my thigh. To my relief, I hadn't broken any limbs. I was able to climb out of the tree and make my way down the overhang to the ravine below."

Rashid told them he found his hunting rifle and cell phone lying broken on the rocks at the bottom. It was clear the men had wanted his fall to seem accidental. When he looked up, he could see what a narrow escape he had had. Had he been thrown off the plateau four feet to the left or right, he would have met with instant death. The tree on the overhang had saved his life. But there was no way out of the ravine, which was filled with wild animals at night. Even if his hunting rifle worked, he would run out of ammunition soon.

By the position of the sun he could see it was almost mid-afternoon. He knew a search party would not be sent out until they realized he was missing. But no one might think to look for him in the ravine. The wound on his head had stopped bleeding but the gash in his thigh was still dripping blood. He tore a piece of his undershirt and bound it up. He had a painful headache and could feel himself growing weak from the blood loss. He did not know how long he would be able to survive before help came.

As Rashid paused in his tale and looked at the rapt faces around him, he smiled and said, "I prayed and went from corner to corner in the ravine, much like Hajar had done when she was looking for water in the desert for Ishmael. I did find a small stream to quench my thirst and that helped a lot. But the heat combined with blood loss was too much. I was about to collapse in exhaustion when help finally came."

"How?" asked Zahra, her eyes wide.

"I heard a helicopter flying above the ravine."

"A helicopter?!" came a chorus of exclamations.

"Yes, it was flying low and I had to get the attention of the pilot somehow. I took off my shirt and began to wave it in the air as the helicopter came closer and closer to where I stood. When it flew past me, I thought maybe my time on earth was up. But to my joy, it turned around and circled the air above me. Then it came down in the flattest part of the ravine. The pilot and two foreign passengers came out. When the pilot asked me how I got there, I told him I had been pushed over. He looked as if he didn't believe me, so I told him about the tree on the overhang. Shaking his head, he said it was a miracle I had survived."

Rashid told them he had no idea who had tried to kill him.

He had a feeling it had something to do with the anonymous letters he had been receiving. He suspected they were being sent by someone in the household. He could not take the chance of going back to the castle. He would be exposing himself to the killer again. He decided to stay in hiding until he could find out who his unknown enemy was. With that plan in mind, he threw his bloodied shirt on the rocks, close to where his rifle and cell phone had landed. He knew everyone would assume he had been eaten by the wild animals in the ravine. Clad in his torn undershirt, he was helped into the helicopter where the two passengers made room for him. The pilot asked him where he wanted to go. Thinking where he would be safe, he found the ideal hiding place.

"Where?" asked Adam.

"With a group of nomadic *bedu* herdsmen who had set up camp outside of Khaldun. I've helped them in the past and knew they were a trustworthy tribe. When we got there, I told the pilot who I was and promised him a generous reward for keeping silent until I found out who wanted me dead. He promised and told me I didn't have to worry about the passengers. They were Swedish geologists employed by a mining company to look for oil and would be leaving Ghassan in a few days. After the helicopter left, I was surrounded by the *bedu* who were curious to know what was going on. I met with the council of elders and told them my tale. They agreed to grant me protection for as long as I needed it. After taking care of my wounds and giving me clothes to wear, it was like I had become one of them. I was hiding in plain sight but still close to the castle."

After Rashid had spent a week recovering from his wounds and gaining full strength, he was ready to contact someone at the castle who would help him. The person he chose was Hatem. Through the *bedu*, he sent a message, asking Hatem to meet him in the night outside the castle wall. All other meetings took place there.

"Dressed the way I was, rumors soon began flying around Khaldun that the Hooded Horseman was back," Rashid concluded.

"But why did you think you could trust Hatem?" asked Jumana.

It was Hatem who answered. "Because I was the original Hooded Horseman. After Rashid saved my life, he knew he could trust me with his."

Chapter Twenty-Eight
To Catch a Scorpion

"You were the Hooded Horseman?" asked Hala. "How did you become him?"

Hatem sighed. "It's a long, painful story. It began two and a half years ago when I crossed paths with *Al-Aqrab*. I saw a young boy being kidnapped. I was able to stop the kidnapper and rescue the boy. The boy was the son of a wealthy merchant in the city. The kidnapper was arrested, and I was called to testify as a witness at the forthcoming trial. That's when I started receiving threatening letters telling me not to testify or I would regret it."

Hatem told them even though he was afraid, he ignored the letters because they needed his evidence at the trial. When he returned home after the trial, he found his wife and three-year-old daughter dead. They had been stung by two scorpions, which were also lying dead next to them.

"That's the story the gypsy woman told us about," said Zahra. "It was *Al-Aqrab's* work."

"At that time, I didn't know he was responsible," said Hatem. "But I knew their deaths weren't accidental. There were signs they had been tied and gagged. The gags and ropes were taken off after they died to make their deaths appear accidental."

They could see the grief on Hatem's face as he recalled the hurtful memories.

"How did you learn *Al-Aqrab* was responsible?" asked Zaid.

"I visited the kidnapper in prison and begged him to tell me who had murdered an innocent woman and child. With great fear in his eyes, he whispered, '*Al-Aqrab*.' No matter how much I begged him, he could tell me nothing else. The police didn't have the faintest idea who *Al-Aqrab* was. Filled with anger, I was determined to find this killer myself. In the nights I became the Hooded Horseman to find out what I could. During that time, I helped some people, so the Hooded Horseman became known as a good guy. But I had learned nothing of *Al-Aqrab*. No one seemed to know who he was except the man in prison. One night, a gypsy man came to me and said he knew someone who could tell me about *Al-Aqrab*. But the person wanted such and such amount of money. I told him I was willing to pay but not until I got the information I wanted. I knew better than to be taken in by some trick. He came back to tell me the meeting had been set for eleven the next night by the racetrack. When I got there, I was attacked by two men with knives."

"It was a trap," said Adam.

"Yes, and I was unprepared. I had a hunting rifle in my horse's saddle but couldn't get to it. I had learned some judo moves and defended myself at the start. When both attackers came at me with their knives from opposite directions, I leaped aside. They ran into each other and one of them was stabbed to death by the other's knife. In a fury, the remaining attacker came at me with the knife, slashing all over my body. He caused the most damage to my face." Hatem ran a finger over his scar. "After I blacked out, my assailant took me into the desert so wild animals and vultures could finish me off. Luckily, his knife had missed my vital organs. I recovered consciousness in time to stop more loss of blood. But I would have died if Rashid hadn't found me the next morning when he rode into the desert. He took me to the hospital and I slowly recovered from my wounds. After I came out, I learned that *Al-Aqrab* was circulating stories that the Hooded Horseman had killed someone. I knew if I continued looking for *Al-Aqrab*, my life would be in danger again. That's why I gave it up. When Rashid offered me a position at the stables, I accepted. And that's my story."

"Wow, what a tale," said Layla.

Rashid said, "When I met with Hatem for the first time outside the grove, I asked him to get in touch with the same private investigator I had been planning to bring from Ghassan City. But the investigator was out of the country and would not return until the end of August. Since there was nothing else I could do, I decided to remain in hiding. I would see what Hatem and I could dig up in the meantime. We met several times but still had no idea who wanted me dead. When Hatem told me about the stone in Tariq's saddle, I became worried. Even more so when he told me he heard the young guests and Tariq talking about *Al-Aqrab*. I started keeping watch on the castle's gates at night. I wanted to make sure no strangers were going in. That's how I saw Jumana being kidnapped and rescued her. When you rode out to the desert, Hatem was worried and came to the *bedu* camp to tell me. I went after you, trying to keep out of sight. I think you saw me by the dunes."

"We did," said Tariq. "I thought you were a *bedu* herdsman."

"How did you know we were in the caves today?" asked Zahra.

"Hatem sent one of the grooms with a message. I knew it would be dangerous, so I took a rifle and knife. I used a different route to get into the caves. I let the two men guarding the entrance see me when I got inside. They chased after me, but I hid from them. They went to tell their other two men. When they all came searching for me, I lured them into the cave that had the shaft. I had almost fallen into it once myself, that's how I knew where it was."

"Lucky for us," said Zaid. "Allah knows what *Al-Aqrab* would have done to us all."

The young people then took turns telling their side of the tale and when they were done, Shaykh Sulaiman said, "Oh, Suha, Suha. She was seduced by Satan. Poor Lamis, what a grievous wrong was done to her."

Nura looked like a great weight had been lifted off her shoulders. "Lamis told me once she was very close to one of her aunts who had no children of her own. That aunt loved her like her own daughter. She must have been talking about Mrs. Haddad."

"Suha said *Al-Aqrab* was your own blood," said Layla. "Who could she have meant?"

"There's only one person here that fits the bill." Tariq looked at Faisal.

All eyes swung to Faisal.

"You think I'm *Al-Aqrab?*" he said.

"Layla heard you on the phone one day in your suite," said Tariq. "You were telling someone you will hold up your end of the deal, no matter the cost."

Layla blushed as Faisal stared at her in displeasure. "I'm not even going to ask what you were doing in my suite, young lady. The time has now come for me to reveal why I've been going to Khaldun so often. It's because I'm embarking on an important business partnership. I had to keep it under wraps at the request of the investors until the plan was finalized. We were able to finalize it this morning. It has nothing to do with this *Al-Aqrab* you're talking about."

"There's a way to find out if Faisal is *Al-Aqrab* or not," said Zahra. "Remember the clue we got from the gypsy woman?"

"Yes, Zahra's right," said Zaid.

Turning to Faisal, Tariq said, "To prove you're not *Al-Aqrab*, can you take off your shirt for us?"

"Take off my shirt," Faisal echoed. "You're not serious, are you?"

"I'm very serious," said Tariq.

"This is ridiculous," Faisal growled. "What mumbo jumbo did that gypsy woman tell you?"

"I would advise you to listen to them," said Rashid. "They're very smart kids."

"Fine." Faisal relented. "I have no idea what you hope to find." He stood up and removed his gray cotton T-shirt, revealing a sleeveless white undershirt beneath. And no sign of a tattoo.

"It's not there," said Layla, feeling relieved for Shaykh Sulaiman's sake that Faisal was not the killer.

"I guess Faisal is not *Al-Aqrab,*" said Zaid.

"Or the gypsy woman could have lied about the tattoo," said Kareem. "The gypsies are notorious for telling lies."

The teenagers realized at once the significance of the PA's words.

"Kareem must be *Al-Aqrab,*" cried Zahra. "We didn't mention a tattoo at all, but he knew."

Kareem looked blindsided by his blunder. The next moment, he leaped to his feet and pulled out a gun. There were gasps of fear all around.

"No one leaves this room," he said. "Or you're going to die."

Hatem looked dazed. "All along, you were right under my nose and I had no idea you were *Al-Aqrab*. You must have been laughing behind my back."

"You were just a fly that had to be swatted away. Better men than you have tried to find me," said Kareem.

"Suha lied when she said *Al-Aqrab* was your own blood," said Adam. "Kareem is not related to you."

"Oh, but I am," said Kareem.

Shaykh Sulaiman frowned. "Explain yourself."

"In the eyes of the world, I'm not an Al-Khalili. My father denied me my heritage before I was even born. But it doesn't change who I am. I still have Al-Khalili blood flowing through my veins."

"Uncle Husam's son," Tariq gasped. "Suha's half-brother."

"Oh, my goodness," Layla exclaimed. "It all makes sense now. Kareem and Suha were the ones arguing in the grove that night."

"You're Uncle Husam's son?" Shaykh Sulaiman whispered, looking frail and tired again.

"Yes, I'm Husam's son," said Kareem. "Since I was a child, my mother told me how my father abandoned us for another woman. She wouldn't tell me who he was, though I asked her many times. We were so poor that when I was a teenager I was recruited by a wealthy and powerful man, who was the first *Al-Aqrab*. He told me he would groom me to be his successor. I went to university, got a good education and lived an outwardly respectable life. When he died seven years ago, I took over as *Al-Aqrab*. Then my mother became sick. On her deathbed, she finally told me who my father was and gave me the marriage certificate. I was disgusted that it was Husam, the black sheep of the Al-Khalili family. I vowed to make him pay for what he had done to my mother. But then I found out he had died. I was denied my revenge. When I saw the advertisement for the position of Personal Assistant to Sulaiman, it occurred to me that I could take my revenge on the Al-Khalilis if I got the position. I applied and got it. Ironically, my very first assignment was to search for Husam's *bedu* wife and child. I knew he had died penniless and there was nothing in it for me. I didn't want the Al-Khalilis to know who I was until I had figured out what my revenge would be. It was easy to give Sulaiman wrong information that mother and child couldn't be found."

"It wasn't the fault of the Al-Khalilis that Uncle Husam left your mother," said Rashid. "We knew nothing of her until he told us on his deathbed. The blame lies only with him."

"How dare you involve Suha in your evil schemes." Miftah's voice trembled with rage.

"She became quite fond of me after I told her I was her half-brother. She was angry she had been scorned by Rashid and had come to regret marrying you. We put our heads together to come up with a plan of revenge."

"Why were you determined on revenge?" asked Shaykh Sulaiman. "Had you told us who you were, we would have welcomed you with open arms."

Kareem's lips curled with disdain. "I didn't want your pity and just a few dirhams. As a cousin, I knew I would only get a measly bequest like the others. I wanted the Al-Khalili fortune. Once I got it, I would stop being *Al-Aqrab*. After we found out Mrs. Haddad was the Woman in White we came up with the grand scheme. But it has come to naught now."

"What was your grand scheme?" asked Rashid.

Kareem gave an unpleasant chuckle. "It would have taken place at the farewell dinner for Tariq. Sulaiman was planning it as a surprise two days before Tariq leaves for England. For the grand scheme to work, we needed Sulaiman to be at the dinner table. That's why we couldn't do it earlier. Here's what would have happened. Mrs. Haddad gets her revenge for her niece's death by sneaking into the dining room before the farewell dinner and putting large doses of the lethal poison ricin in the soup. After poisoning the soup, Mrs. Haddad pretends to have a migraine and does not go down to dinner. Everyone at the table drinks the soup, except for Suha, who will give some reason for not doing so. Tragedy strikes when the Al-Khalilis who drink the soup are poisoned to death. When the police come, they find Mrs. Haddad dead. She has injected herself with a fatal dose of the painkiller she has stolen from Qais's supplies. Most important, they find a typed confession in her room, saying she was the Woman in White and has now avenged her niece's death. Of course, I would have been the one to put the poison in the soup and steal the painkiller from Qais. Suha would have been the one to inject Mrs. Haddad with the painkiller and plant the fake confession in her room."

"Where would you have been while the Al-Khalilis are drinking the poisoned soup?" asked Layla.

"I would have left the dinner table at the beginning of the meal to take an urgent phone call. Imagine my horror when I'm called to the dining room to deal with the dying Al-Khalilis and a hysterical Suha. I would have acted the grieving employee. After a decent amount of time, I would then reveal I was Husam's son and Sulaiman made me promise not to tell anyone. I already have the marriage certificate and a DNA test in my possession that proves I'm related to Sulaiman by blood. There would have been no objection to my rightful claim to the Al-Khalili fortune. But everything fell apart when you kids came. I was hoping your visit would have been canceled because of Rashid's supposed death but Sulaiman didn't want to disappoint you. And then Jumana came too. And soon, your parents would have showed up. It would have messed up the whole plan."

"I didn't think you would give a damn about a few more bodies," said Faisal.

"I might have been able to fool the bungling police around these parts, but I didn't want the American authorities and Jumana's father to become involved. They might have found out the truth. Suha told me I was being a fool and they would never find out. She finally convinced me we should go ahead with the scheme regardless of who was here. If all had gone according to plan, you would all have been dead in two weeks' time."

"You were going to poison us all in two weeks?" screeched Ghazala.

Kareem smirked. "I'm afraid so."

Layla suddenly felt ill.

Shaykh Sulaiman said to Kareem, "You have shamed the name of Al-Khalili just like your father did."

Kareem shrugged. "I gave it the best shot I could, but the odds weren't in my favor. Now, I've talked enough. I want you all to stay here and don't make a move while I leave."

His cell phone rang at that moment. Distracted by the sound, his gaze moved away from the family. Quick as a wink, Rashid and Faisal sprang at him, trying to get the gun away. The gun went off with a bang. Faisal gave a cry of pain as he fell to the ground. There were squeals of fear all around. The head groom and the nurse now helped Rashid to subdue Kareem. The gun went off twice more, hitting the wall and the floor before the men were able to restrain Kareem.

The other servants from the household appeared, looking frightened. Dhul Fikar was sent to call for the police and an ambulance. Faisal's right upper arm was bleeding and his face looked very white. They were relieved the bullet had not hit any of his vital parts.

Qais got his nursing supplies and bandaged the arm. A servant brought ropes and Kareem was bound up, his face looking savage. With a choked cry, Miftah launched himself at their newly-discovered cousin, trying to grab him by the throat. Rashid and Qais wrested him away and returned him to the sofa, where he cried like a child, Hala and Ghazala trying to console him.

The ambulance and police came together. Faisal was lifted into the ambulance and driven away. As the police were about to lead Kareem away, only then did a look of remorse appear on the PA's face. "I have one request to make."

"You're not deserving of any request," said the Shaykh.

"But my family is," said Kareem. "My wife and children are innocent of the actions of *Al-Aqrab*. Since the children share your blood, I would like you to become their guardian."

Shaykh Sulaiman sighed. "It's not my intention to punish

the innocent. I'll make sure your family don't suffer the consequences of your actions."

After the police left, everyone was still talking in the domed hall.

"But wouldn't the soup have smelled funny?" asked Hala. "I'm sure I wouldn't have eaten it if it did."

"Ricin is odorless and tasteless," said Qais. "You wouldn't have smelled or tasted any difference. But it causes a very painful death."

Ghazala shuddered. "Thank Allah for these young people being here. Imagine being poisoned to death in such a horrible way."

Epilogue

TWO WEEKS LATER, the forecourt of the castle, cleared of vehicles and crammed with colorful tents and decorative streamers, was teeming with well-wishers who had come to celebrate the wedding of Jumana and Rashid. The *nikaah* had been held earlier that afternoon. Layla had been moved to tears to witness the couple finally being united after the trials they had overcome. In light of the recent events, it had been a low key ceremony. There was just a small gathering of family and close friends.

To Layla and Zahra's delight, Jumana had chosen them, along with Hala, to be her bridesmaids. The three girls were dressed in identical peach gowns with gold-colored scarves. The *walimah*, or wedding feast, had begun right after the congratulatory speeches were over. Laughter and the merry sound of voices filled the air as the guests now enjoyed the buffet of delicious food and desserts that had been laid out for them.

As Layla ate, she reflected on the events of the last two weeks.

The day after the showdown in the caves, Suha and Mrs. Haddad's bodies had been recovered from the bowels of the earth and given quick burials. Shaykh Sulaiman had sent someone posthaste to England to meet with Mrs. Haddad's family to explain what had happened and compensate them for the loss of another family member.

The bullet had been removed from Faisal's arm and he was back home and recovering. His brush with death had changed him. He was quiet and thoughtful these days. Tariq had told them there was also another reason for this change. Faisal had found out that Suha was the one responsible for breaking up his marriage. She had told him his wife had been unfaithful with Rashid. It had led to a rift between the two men. While Faisal was recovering in the hospital, he finally asked Rashid about it. Rashid denied it as another of Suha's lies and Faisal was now thinking of reconciling with his wife.

Shaykh Sulaiman had the unpleasant task of revealing to Kareem's wife the double life her husband had led. Tariq, who had accompanied his grandfather and Rashid on that mission, told his new friends that his heart had gone out to the family when he had seen the devastating hurt on their faces. Shaykh Sulaiman was making arrangements for Kareem's wife and teenage children, two girls and a boy, to come live at Dukhan Castle.

Layla knew it would take time for the family to recover from the shock of Kareem's deceit. Shaykh Sulaiman had vowed to protect the children as much as possible from the fallout resulting from the actions of their father's evil alter ego, *Al-Aqrab*. The Mole Man and the rest of the accomplices from the caves had been arrested. The Tri-Country Bureau of Inquiries were still trying to round up all those who had belonged to the evil network. And Rashid had duly rewarded the pilot of the helicopter who had rescued him from the ravine.

Traumatized by what had happened, Hala seemed to have gained a newfound maturity and had become a great source of consolation to her heartbroken *Abu*. She had apologized to Layla for her previous behavior. She also said she was looking forward to moving to Ghassan City with her father and then going to university. She had made no mention of Tariq. Layla guessed the other girl had learned a bitter lesson from her stepmother. Suha had destroyed her own life because of the grudge she held against Rashid for not marrying her.

Jumana's bracelet was found hidden in Suha's room. It was given to Ghazala since Jumana no longer wanted it. Tariq, though looking forward to university, was sad to be leaving the castle and his remaining family. He cheered up when Rashid and Jumana promised to visit him frequently in England.

The castle's employees sat together, Hatem and Nura among them. Layla grinned when she thought of the latest gossip they had heard over the castle's grapevine. After a whirlwind wooing, the head groom had proposed to their maid and she had accepted. The two were planning to move to Ghassan City after they were married. Hatem would be trying his hand at managing an Al-Khalili hotel instead of grooming horses while Nura would attend university. The teenagers were glad that Hatem was getting married again after what he had been through, and that Nura would have the education she desired.

Layla looked at the table where her parents were conversing with Shaykh Sulaiman and Zaid and Zahra's parents. The Alkurdis and Horanis had arrived two days prior. Her twin brothers, Hassan and Hakeem, had been over the moon at finally seeing Shaykh Sulaiman's desert castle. In the two days since their arrival, they had gotten into so many scrapes that Layla shuddered to think what would have happened had they come sooner.

As expected, their parents had been stunned to hear of their escapades.

"You children seem to be magnets for attracting trouble," Mrs. Horani had said, shaking her head in bemusement. "This is the second time you've been on the trail of villains."

"Unbelievable and quite distressing," Professor Alkurdi had added.

"Our parents won't let us out of their sight now after hearing of our latest adventure," said Adam.

"Yes, they were quite shocked, poor things," said Zahra.

Zaid grinned. "Maybe our next vacation will be a quiet one, *insha Allah.*"

Layla said, "I wouldn't hold my breath on that one."

Glossary

Abaya: A loose overgarment worn by some Muslim women

Abu: Father

Al-Aqrab: The Scorpion

Allah: The Arabic name for God

Assalaam Alaikum: Peace be unto you; the first greeting that Muslims say to each other

Bedu: Bedouin

Domari: A language spoken by gypsies

Dukhan: Smoke

Eid: Either of the two festivals celebrated by Muslims

Falafel: A deep-fried ball, or a flat or doughnut-shaped patty, made from ground chickpeas, fava beans, or both

Ghaf: A drought-tolerant evergreen tree found in the Middle East

Ghul: Ghoul

Habibi: My beloved

Haboob: An intense sandstorm or dust storm

Hijab: The clothing that some Muslim women wear that leaves only the hands and face uncovered and, in some instances, only the hands uncovered

Imam: The prayer leader of a mosque

Insha Allah: If Allah (God) wills

Jinn: An unseen being created out of fire that can do both good and harm to mankind

Jumu'ah: The Friday prayer, required for men to be prayed in congregation

Kanafeh: Traditional Arab dessert made with thin, noodle-like pastry

Kebab: A cooked meat dish with many variants in Muslim countries

Khalas: Enough

Kibbeh: A dish made of finely ground beef, lamb, goat or camel meat

Kohl: Eye cosmetic that darkens the eyes

Kofta: A family of meatball or meatloaf dishes

Majlis-al-jinn: The meeting place of the jinn

La: No

Marhaban: Welcome

Masah-al- khair: Good night

Na'am: Yes

Najd: A geographical central region of Saudi Arabia

Nikaah: Muslim wedding ceremony

Qasabah: A single stone tower

Qur'an: The Holy Book of the Muslims and the last of the

revealed books from God sent through revelation to the Prophet Muhammad (on whom be peace)

Samak-Baladi: Country-style fish

Shamal: A hot, dry northwesterly wind blowing across the Persian Gulf in summer, typically causing sandstorms

Sharih Lubabah: The street of innermost essence

Shaykh: An Arabic title for a knowledgeable and/or respected person

Shawarma: Meat cut in thin slices and stacked in a cone-like shape on a vertical rotisserie

Souk: Market

Ta'al: Come

Wa Alaikum Assalaam: And unto you, be peace; the return greeting for *Assalaam Alaikum*

Coming Next!

Book Three:
The Hour of the Oryx

Follow at:
https://www.farahzamanauthor.com
FB: @farahzamanauthor
IG: @farahzamanauthor
Email: Zefarah@gmail.com

CPSIA information can be obtained
at www.ICGtesting.com
Printed in the USA
LVHW091539031121
702350LV00015B/85

9 781945 873140